William Allingham

Fifty modern Poems

William Allingham

Fifty modern Poems

ISBN/EAN: 9783743333840

Manufactured in Europe, USA, Canada, Australia, Japa

Cover: Foto ©Andreas Hilbeck / pixelio.de

Manufactured and distributed by brebook publishing software (www.brebook.com)

William Allingham

Fifty modern Poems

FIFTY MODERN POEMS.

BY

WILLIAM ALLINGHAM.

TO A. F.

Dear F.

My " Works," for so far, (trivial enough works!) are now in three volumes, containing a hundred and thirteen poems, long and short. These claim to be genuine in their way, and beyond this the writer thinks or cares very little about them ; but it emboldens him to ask you to accept the present little book, and to continue to think kindly of

Your Friend.

March. 1865

CONTENTS.

		Page
I.	INVITATION to a Painter	1
II.	Song. " We Two"	15
III.	George Levison; or, the Schoolfellows	17
IV.	The Old Sexton	30
V.	Recovery	32
VI.	The Shooting Star	33
VII. "	On the Longest Day"	35
VIII.	Abbey Asaroe	38
IX.	Late Autumn	42
X.	Robin Redbreast	43
XI.	Sir Hugh de la Pole	45
XII.	Song	49
XIII.	In Weimar	50
XIV.	Every Day	54
XV.	The Lapracaun, or Fairy Shoemaker	57
XVI.	After Sunset	61
XVII.	Southwell Park	62
XVIII.	The Little Dell	85
XIX.	A Wife	88
XX.	Old Master Grunsey and Goodman Dodd	90
XXI.	The Poor Little Maiden	98
XXII. "	Across the Sea"	101
XXIII.	His Town	103
XXIV.	Hymn	105
XXV.	The Queen of the Forest	106

A 2

viii   *Contents.*

		Page
XXVI.	Progress	109
XXVII.	The Winding Banks of Erne; or, the Emigrant's Adieu to Ballyshannon	111
XXVIII.	Loss	119
XXIX.	Winter Verdure	121
XXX.	A Dream of a Gate	122
XXXI.	Danger	130
XXXII.	The Abbot of Innisfallen	131
XXXIII.	Sunday Bells	137
XXXIV.	Two Fairies in a Garden	139
XXXV.	Emily	147
XXXVI.	Nightwind	150
XXXVII.	Winter Cloud	152
XXXVIII.	Evening Prayer	153
XXXIX.	A Vernal Voluntary	154
XL.	A Gravestone	159
XLI.	Angela	160
XLII.	The Mowers	163
XLIII.	Dogmatism	166
XLIV.	Æolian Harp	168
XLV.	Among the Heather	170
XLVI.	Two Moods	172
XLVII.	Mea Culpa	175
XLVIII.	Down on the Shore	177
XLIX.	To the Nightingales	179
L.	" These little Songs "	182

NOTE. Six of these poems, XIV, XXXIII, XXXIV, XXXVI, XLI, XLIII, appeared in an early volume, out of print some years.

FIFTY MODERN POEMS.

I.

INVITATION TO A PAINTER.

1.

FLEE from London, good my Walter! boundless jail of bricks and gas;
Care not if your Exhibition swarm with portrait
and Gil Blas,
Or with marvels dear to Ruskin; fly the swelter, fly
the crush,
British Mammon in his glory,—in his breathless
race and rush.
Leave the hot tumultuous city for the breakers'
rival roar,
Quit your soft suburban landscape for the rude hills
by the shore,

Leagues of smoke for morning vapour lifted off a
  mountain-range,
Crinoline for barefoot beauty, and for " something
  new and strange "
All your towny wit and gossip.   You shall both in
  field and fair,
Paddy's cunning and politeness with the Cockney
  ways compare,
Catch those lilts and old-world tunes the maidens
  at their needle sing,
Peep at dancers, from an outskirt of the blithe
  applausive ring,
See our petty Court of Justice, where the swearing's
  very strong.
See our little plain St. Peter's with its kneeling
  peasant throng;
Hear the brogue and Gaelic round you; sketch a
  hundred Irish scenes,
Not more whisky and shillelagh—wedding bac-
  ques, funeral *keenes*;
Rove at pleasure, noon or midnight; change you
  with all you meet;
Ten times safer than in England, far less trammelled
  in your feet.

Here, the only danger known
Is walking where the land's your own.
Landscape-lords are left alone.

2.

We are barren, I confess it; but our scope of view
    is fine;
Dignifying shapes of mountains wave on each
    horizon-line.
So withdrawn that never house-room utmost pomp
    of cloud may lack,
Dawn or sunset, moon or planet, or mysterious
    zodiac.
Hills beneath run all a-wrinkle, rocky, moory,
    pleasant green;
From its Lough the Flood descending, flashes like
    a sword between,
Through our crags and woods and meadows, to the
    mounded harbour-sand,
To the Bay, calm blue, or, sometimes, whose
    Titanic arms expand
Welcome to the mighty billow rolling in from
    Newfoundland.

Oats, potatoes, cling in patches round the rocks
    and boulder-stones,
Like a motley ragged garment for the lean Earth's
    jutting bones;
Moors extend, and bogs and furzes, where you
    seldom meet a soul,
But the Besom-man or woman, who to earn a stingy
    dole
Stoops beneath a nodding burden of the scented
    heather-plant,
Or a jolly gaiter'd Sportsman, striding near the
    grouse's haunt,
Slow the anchoritic heron, musing by his voiceless
    pond,
Startled, with the startled echo on the lonely cliff
    beyond,
Rising, flaps away.   And now a summit shows us,
    wide and bare,
All the brown uneven country, lit with waters here
    and there;
Southward, mountains—northward, mountains—
    westward, golden mystery
Of coruscation, when the Daystar flings his largess
    on the sea;

Peasant cots with humble haggarts; mansions with
    obsequious groves:
A Spire, a Steeple, rival standards, which the
    liberal distance loves
To set in union. There the dear but dirty little
    Town abides,
And you and I come home to dinner after all our
    walks and rides.
    You shall taste a cleanly pudding;
    But, bring shoes to stand a mudding.

3.

Let me take you by the *murragh*, sprinkled with
    the Golden Weeds
Merry troops of Irish Fairies mount by moonlight
    for their steeds, —
Wherefore sacred and abundant over all the land
    are they.
Many cows are feeding through it; cooling, of a
    sultry day,

" Murvagh," level place near the sea, salt marsh.
" Golden Weeds," ragwort, called " boughdeen bwee,"
(little yellow boy), also " fairy-horse."

By the River's brink, that journeys under Fairy
　　Hill, and past
Gentle cadences of landscape sloping to the sea at
　　last.
Now the yellow sand is round us, drifted in fantastic
　　shapes,
Heights and hollows, forts and bastions, pyramids
　　and curving capes,
Breezy ridges thinly waving with the bent-weed's
　　pallid green,
Delicate for eye that sips it, till a better feast is
　　seen
Where the turf swells thick-embroider'd with the
　　fragrant purple thyme,
Where, in plots of speckled orchis, poet larks begin
　　their rhyme,
Honey'd galium wafts an invitation to the gypsy
　　bees,
Rabbits' doorways wear for garlands azure tufts of
　　wild heartsease,
Paths of sward around the hillocks, dipping into
　　ferny dells,
Show you heaps of childhood's treasure—twisted,
　　vary-tinted shells

Lapt in moss and blossoms, empty, and forgetful
  of the wave.

Ha! a creature scouring nimbly, hops at once into
  his cave;

Brother Coney sits regardant,—wink an eye, and
  where is he?

Towns and villages we pass through, but the people
  skip and flee.

Over sandy slope, a Mountain lifts afar his fine
  blue head;

There the savage twins of eagles, gaping, hissing
  to be fed,

Welcome back their wide-wing'd parent with a
  rabbit scarcely dead

Hung in those powerful yellow claws, and gorge
  the bloody flesh and fur

On ledge of rock, their cradle. Shepherd-boy!
  with limbs and voice bestir

To your watch of tender lambkins on a lonesome
  valley-side,

If you, careless in the sunshine, see a rapid shadow
  glide

Down the verdant undercliff. Afar that conquering
  eye can sweep

Mountain-glens, and *moy*, and warren, to the
     margin of the deep,

Worse than dog or ferret,—vanish from your gold-
     green-mossy dells,

Nibbling natives of the burrow! seek your inmost
     winding cells

     When such cruelties appear:

     But a Painter do not fear,

     Nor a Poet, loitering near.

4.

Painter, what is spread before you? 'Tis the great
     Atlantic sea!

Many-colour'd floor of ocean, where the lights and
     shadows flee;

Waves and wavelets running landward with a
     sparkle and a song,

Crystal green with foam enwoven, bursting, brightly
     spilt along:

Thousand living shapes of wonder in the clear
     pools of the rock:

Lengths of strand, and seafowl armies rising like a
    puff of smoke;

Drift and tangle on the limit where the wandering
    water fails ;

Level faintly-clear horizon, touch'd with clouds and
    phantom sails, -

O come hither! weeks together let us watch the
    big Atlantic,

Blue or purple, green or gurly, dark or shining,
    smooth or frantic.

Far across the tide, slow-heaving, rich autumnal
    daylight sets ;

See our crowd of busy row-boats, hear us noisy
    with our nets,

Where the glittering sprats in millions from the
    rising mesh are stript,

Till there scarce is room for rowing, every gunwale
    nearly dipt :

Gulls around us, flying, dropping, thick in air as
    flakes of snow,

Snatching luckless little fishes in their silvery over-
    flow.

Now one streak of western scarlet lingers upon
    ocean's edge,

Now through ripples of the splendour of the moon
    we swiftly wedge
Our loaded bows: the fisher-hamlet beacons with
    domestic light:
On the shore the carts and horses wait to travel
    through the night
To a distant city market, while the boatmen sup
    and sleep,
While the firmamental stillness arches o'er the
    dusky deep,
    Ever muttering chaunts and dirges
    Round its rocks and sandy verges.

5.

Ere we part at winter's portal. I shall row you of
    night
On a swirling Stygian river, to a ghostly yellow
    light.
When the nights are black and gusty, then deeds
    in myriads glide
Through the pools and down the rapids, hurrying
    to the ocean-tide,—

But they fear the frost or moonshine, in their
    mud-beds coiling close—
And the wearmen, on the platform of that pigmy
    water-house
Built among the river-currents, with a dam to either
    bank,
Pull the purse-net's heavy end to swing across their
    wooden tank,
Ere they loose the cord about it—then a slimy
    wriggling heap
Falls with splashing, where a thousand fellow-
    prisoners heave and creep.
Chill winds roar above the wearmen, darkling rush
    the floods below :
There they watch and work their eel-nets, till the
    late dawn lets them go.
There we'll join their eely supper, bearing smoke the
    best we can,
(House's furniture a salt-box, truss of straw, and
    frying-pan),
Hearken Con's astounding stories, Low a mytho-
    logical
Chased a man o'er miles of country, swallow'd two
    dogs at a meal,

To the hissing bubbling music of the pan and
  pratie-pot.
Denser grows the reek around us, each like
  Mussulman a-squat,
Each with victuals in his fingers, we devour them
  hot and hot;
  Smoky rays our lantern throwing,
  Ruddy peat-fire warmly glowing,
  Noisily the River flowing.

6.

But first of all—the time's at hand to journey to
  our Holy Well.
Clear as when the old Saint bless'd it, rising in its
  rock-bound cell.
Two great Crosses, carved in bosses, curves, and
  fillets interlacing,
Spread their aged arms of stone, as if in sempiternal
  blessing;
Five much-wriakled thorntrees bend, as though in
  everlasting pray'r,
Greenly shines the growing crop, along the shelter'd
  hill-side there;

But the tristful little Abbey, crumbling among
    weeds and grass,
Nevermore can suns or seasons bring a smile to us
    they pass;
By a window-gap or mullion creeps the fringe of
    ivy leaves,
Nettles crowd the sculptured doorway, where the
    wind goes through and grieves;
Sad the tender blue of harebells on its ledges low
    and high;
Merry singing of the goldfinch there sounds pensive
    as a sigh.

'Tis a day of summer: see you, how the pilgrims
    wend along:
Scarlet petticoat, blue mantle, grey frieze, mingling
    in the throng.
By the pathway sit the Beggars, each an ailment
    and a whine:
Lame and sickly figures pass them, tottering in that
    pilgrim line:
Children carried by their parents, very loth to let
    them die;
Lovely girls too, with their eyelids downcast on a
    rosary;

Shrunken men. and witch-like women; young men
    in their proudest prime:
Guilty foreheads, hot-blood faces, penance-vow'd
    for secret crime.
All by turn, in slow procession, pace the venerable
    bounds,
Barefoot, barehead, seven times duly kneeling in
    th' accustom'd rounds:
Thrice among the hoary ruins, once before the
    wasted shrine,
Once at each great carven cross, and once to form
    the Mystic Sign,
Dipping reverential finger in the Well. on brow
    and breast.
Meanwhile worn and wan, the Sick under those
    rooted thorntrees rest,
Waiting sadly. Here are human figures of our land
    and day,
On a thousand-years-old background. still in
    keeping, it and they!
Walter, make a vow nor break it: turn your pilgrim
    steps our way,
    O might you come, before there fell
    On hawthorn-flow'r in Columb's Well!

II.

SONG. "WE TWO."

1.

LET all your looks be grave and cold;
    Or smile upon me still;
And give your hand. or else withhold;
    Take leave howe'er you will.
No lingering trace within your face
    Of love's regard is seen:
We two no more shall be—
    Never -what we've been.

2.

It is not now a longing day
    Divides us, nor a year;
Your heart from mine has turn'd away,
    Nor henceforth sheds a tear.

The winter snow may come and go,
  And April shadows green :
We two no more shall be—
  Never—what we've been.

3.

Ah never!   countless hours that bring
  Full many a chance and change,
May choose a beggar-boy for king,
  Or cleave a mountain-range.
The salt-sea tide may yet be dried
  That rolls far lands between :
We two no more can be -
  Never—what we've been.

III.

GEORGE LEVISON:

OR, THE SCHOOLFELLOWS.

THE noisy sparrows in our clematis
    Chatted of rain, a pensive summer dusk
Shading the little lawn and garden-ground
Between our threshold and the village-street;
With one pure star, a lonely altar-lamp
In twilight's vast cathedral.   But the clouds
Were gravely gathering, and a fitful breeze
Flurried the window-foliage that before
Hung delicately painted on the sky,
And wafted, showering from their golden boss,
The white-rose petals.
           On the garden side
Our wall being low, the great Whiterose-bush lean'd
A thousand tender little heads, to note

The doings of the village all day long;
From when the labourers, trudging to their toil
In earliest sunshine, heard the outpost cocks
Whistle a quaint refrain from farm to farm,
Till hour of shadow, silence, and repose,
The ceasing footstep, and the taper's light.
Up to the churchyard rail, down to the brook,
And lifted fields beyond with grove and hedge,
The Rose-bush gazed; and people, as they pass'd,
Aware of sweetness, look'd aloft in turn;
School-children, one arm round a comrade's neck,
Would point to some rich cluster, and repay
A flying bloom with fairer glance of joy.

   In that warm twilight, certain years ago,
At sunset, with the roses in a trance,
And many another blossom fast asleep,
One Flow'r of Flow'rs was closing like the rest.
Night's herald star which look'd across the world
Saw nothing prettier than our little child
Saying his evening prayer at mother's knee,
The white skirt folding on the naked feet,
Too tender for rough ways, his eyes at rest
On his mother's face, a window into heaven.
Kiss'd now, and settled in his cot, he's pleased

With murmuring song, until the large lids droop
And do not rise, and slumber's regular breath
Divides the soft round mouth. So Annie's boy
And mine was laid asleep. I heard her foot
Stir overhead; and hoped there would be time
Before the rain to loiter half an hour,
As far as to the poplars down the road,
And hear the corncrakes through the meadowy vale,
And watch the childhood of the virgin moon,
Above that sunset and its marge of clouds
A floating crescent.

     Sweetheart of my life!—
As then, so now; nay, dearer to me now,
Since love, that fills the soul, expands it too,
And thus it holds more love, and ever more,—
O sweetheart, helpmate, guardian, better self!
Green be those downs and dells above the sea,
Smooth-green for ever, by the plough unhurt,
Nor overdrifted by their neighbouring sands,
Where first I saw you; first since long before
When we were children at an inland place
And play'd together. I had often thought,
I wonder should I know that pleasant child?—
Hardly, I fear'd. I knew her the first glimpse:

While yet the flexile curvature of hat
Kept all her face in shadow to the chin.
And when a breeze to which the harebells danced
Lifted the sun a moment to her eyes,
The ray of recognition flew to mine
Through all the dignity of womanhood.
Like dear old friends we were, yet wondrous new.
The others chatted; she and I not much.
Hearing her ribbon whirring in the wind
(No doubting hopes nor whimsies born as yet)
Was pure felicity, like his who sleeps
Within a sense of some unknown good-fortune,
True, or of dreamland, undetermined which;
My buoyant spirit tranquil in its joy
As the white seamew swinging on the wave.
Since, what vicissitude! We read the past
Bound in a volume, catch the story up
At any leaf we choose, and much forget
How every blind to-morrow was evolved,
How each oracular sentence shaped itself
For after comprehension.
                              Thus I mused,
Then also, in that buried summer dusk,
Rich heavy summer, upon autumn's verge,

My wife and boy upstairs, I leaning grave
Against the window; and through favourite paths
Memory, as one who saunters in a wood,
Found sober joy. In turn that eve itself
Rises distinctly. Troops of dancing moths
Brush'd the dry grass. I heard, as if from far,
The tone of passing voices in the street.
Announced by cheerful octaves of a horn,
Those rapid wheels flew, shaking our white-rose,
That link'd us with the modern Magic-Way,
And all the moving million-peopled world.
For every evening, done our little darg
To keep the threads of life from tanglement,
In happy hour came in the lottery-bag,
Whose messenger had many a prize for us:
The multifarious page ephemeral,
The joy at times of some brave book, whereby
The world is richer; and more special words,
Conveying conjured into dots of ink
Almost the voice, look, gesture that we knew,—
From Annie's former house, or mine, from shore
Of murky Thames, or rarer from hot land
Of Hindoo or Chinese, Canadian woods,
Or that huge isle of kangaroos and gold,

Magnetic metal,—thus to the four winds
One's ancient comrades scatter'd through the world.
Where's Georgy now, I thought, our dread, our pride,
George Levison, the sultan of the school?
With Greek and Latin at those fingers' ends
That sway'd the winning oar and bat; a prince
In pocket-money and accoutrement;
A Cribb in fist, a Cicero in tongue;
Already victor, when his eye should deign
To fix on any summit of success.
For, in his haughty careless way, he'd hint—
" I've got to push my fortune, by-and-bye."
How we all worshipp'd Georgy Levison!
But when I went to college he was gone,
They said to travel, and he took away
Mentor conjoin'd with Crichton from my hopes,—
No trifling blank.   George had done little there,
But could   what could he not? . . . And now
          perhaps.
Some city, in the strangers' burial-ground,
Some desert sand, or hollow under sea,
Hides him without an epitaph.   So men
Slip under, fit to shape the world anew:
And leave their trace—in schoolboy memories.

Then I went thinking how much changed I was
Since those old school-times, not so far away,
Yet now like pre-existence. Can that house,
Those fields and trees, be extant anywhere?
Have not all vanish'd, place, and time, and men?
Or with a journey could I find them all,
And myself with them, as I used to be?
Sore was my battle after quitting these.
No one thing fell as plann'd for; sorrows came
And sat beside me; years of toil went round;
And victory's self was pale and garlandless.
Fog rested on my heart; till softly blew
The wind that clear'd it. 'Twas a simple turn
Of life,—a miracle of heavenly love,
For which, thank God!

     When Annie call'd me up,
We both bent silent, looking at our boy;
Kiss'd unaware (as angels, may be, kiss
Good mortals) on the smoothly rounded cheek,
Turn'd from the window, where a fringe of leaves,
With outlines melting in the darkening blue,
Waver'd and peep'd and whisper'd. Would she
  walk?
Not yet a little were those clouds to stoop

With freshness to the garden and the field.
I waited by our open door; while bats
Flew silently, and musk geranium-leaves
Were fragrant in the twilight that had quench'd
Or tamed the dazzling scarlet of their blooms.
Peace, as of heaven itself, possess'd my heart.
A footstep, not the light step of my wife,
Disturb'd it; then, with slacker pace, a man
Came up beside the porch.   Accosting whom,
And answering to my name: " I fear," he said,
" You'll hardly recollect me now; and yet
We were at school together long ago.
Have you forgotten Georgy Levison?"

He in the red arm-chair; I not far off,
Excited, laughing, waiting for his face:
The first flash of the candles told me all:
Or, if not all, enough, and more.   Those eyes.
When they look'd up at last, were his indeed,
But mesh'd in ugly network, like a snare;
And though his mouth preserved the imperious curve,
Evasion, vacillation, discontent,
Warp'd every feature like a crooked glass.
His hair hung prematurely grey and thin:

From thread-bare sleeves the wither'd tremulous
    hands
Protruded. Why paint every touch of blight?

Tea came. He hurried into ceaseless talk;
Glanced at the ways of many foreign towns;
Knew all those men whose names are on the tongue,
And set their worths punctiliously; brought back
Our careless years; paid Annie compliments
To spare; admired the pattern of the cups;
Landed the cream,—our dairy's, was it not?
A country life was pleasant, certainly,
If one could be content to settle down;
And yet the city had advantages.
He trusted, shortly, underneath his roof
To practise hospitality in turn.
But first to catch the roof, eh? Ha, ha, ha!
That was a business topic he'd discuss
With his old friend by-and-bye—
                For me, I long'd
To hide my face and groan; yet look'd at him;
Opposing pain to grief, presence to thought.

Later, when wine came in, and we two sat

The dreary hours together, how he talk'd!
His schemes of life, his schemes of work and wealth.
Intentions and inventions, plots and plans,
Travels and triumphs, failures, golden hopes.
He was a young man still—had just begun
To see his way.   I knew what he could do
If once he tried in earnest.   He'd return
To Law, next term but one; meanwhile complete
His great work, " *The Philosophy of Life,*
Or, Man's Relation to the Universe,"
The matter lying ready to his hand.
Forty subscribers more, two guineas each,
Would make it safe to publish.   All this time
He fill'd his glass and emptied, and his tongue
Went thick and stammering.   When the wine came
          in
(Perhaps a blame for me—who knows?)   I saw
The glistering eye; a thin and eager hand
Made the decanter chatter on the glass
Like ague.   Could I stop him?   So at last
He wept, and moan'd he was a ruin'd man,
Body and soul; then cursed his enemies
By name, and promised punishment; made vaunt
Of genius, learning; caught my hand again,—

Did I forget my friend—my dear old friend?
Had I a coat to spare? He had no coat
But this one on his back; not one shirt—see!

'Twas all a nightmare; all plain wretched truth.
And how to play physician? Where's the strength
Repairs a slow self-ruin from without?
The fall'n must climb innumerable steps,
With humbleness, and diligence, and pain.
How help him to the first of all that steep?

Midnight was past. I had proposed to find
A lodging near us; for, to say the truth,
I could not bid my wife, for such a guest
In such a plight, prepare the little room
We still call'd " Emma's" from my sister's name.
Then with a sudden mustering up of wits,
And ev'n a touch of his old self, that quick
Melted my heart anew, he signified
His bed was waiting, he would say good-night,
And begg'd me not to stir, he knew his road.
But arm in arm I brought him up the street,
Among the rain-pools, and the pattering drops
Drumming upon our canopy; where few

Or none were out of doors; and once or twice
Some casement from an upper story shed
Penurious lamplight.

　　　　　　Tediously we kept
The morning meal in vain expectancy.
Our box of clothes came back; the people said
He paid without a word, and went his way,
They knew not whither.　He return'd no more.
He now is dead.

　　　　　　Through all the summer-time
The touch of that unhappy visit lay,
Like trace of frost on gardens, on our life.
Great cities give events to every hour;
Not so that ancient village, small, remote,
Half-hid in boscage of a peaceful vale,
With guardian hills, but welcoming the sun,
And every group of seasonable stars
That rise upon the circle of the year:
Open to natural influences; far
From jostling crowds of congregated men.

　That village also lies behind us now:
Midst other fields abide we, other faces.
Annie, my darling, we were happy there,
And Heaven continues happiness and hope

To us and to our children. May their steps
Keep the good pathway through this perilous world.
That village is far-off, that year is fled.
But still, at many a meditative hour
By day or night, or with memorial flash,
I see the ghost of Georgy Levison;
A shifting phantom,—now with boyhood's face
And merry curls; now haggard and forlorn,
As when the candles came into the room.

One sells his soul; another squanders it;
The first buys up the world, the second starves.
Poor George was loser palpably enough;
Supernal Wisdom only knows how much.

IV.

THE OLD SEXTON.

(INSCRIBED TO ALFRED RETHEL.)

'TWAS nigh the hour of evening pray'r:
 The Sexton climb'd his turret-stair,
Wearily, being very old.
The wind of Spring blew fresh and cold,
Wakening there Æolian thrills,
And carrying fragrance from the hills.

From a carven cleft he lean'd,
Eyeing the landscape newly green'd:
The large sun, slowly moving down,
Flash'd the chimneys of the town,—
The same where he was first alive
Eighty years ago and five.

Babe he sees himself, and boy;
Youth, astir with hope and joy;

Wife and wedded love he sees;
Children's children round his knees;
Friends departing one by one;
The graveyard in the setting sun.

He seats him in a stony niche;
The bell-rope sways within his reach;
High in the rafters of the roof
The metal warder hangs aloof;
All the townsfolk wait to hear
That voice they know this many a year.

It is past the ringing hour;
There is silence in the tower;
Save that on a pinnacle
A robin sits, and sings full well.
Hush—at length for prayer they toll:
God receive the parted soul!

V.

RECOVERY.

FOR many a day, like one whose limbs are stiff,
Whose head is heavy with some grievous ail,
I felt, from wicked thoughts, the whole world drag
As millstone round my neck, all my force fail,
Dry up, and ravel into dust and rag.
But lo, I slept, and waking glad as if
I had been hearing music in my sleep,
Went forth, and look'd upon thy watery deep,
O King Unseen! By stretch of some great hand
My sad, confused, fearful soul was shriv'n:
I knew the tranquil mind restored to me
To enjoy the colour of that pure blue heav'n,
Purply cloud-shadows on the greenish sea,
And rippling white foam on the yellow sand.

VI.

THE SHOOTING STAR.

1.

AUTUMNAL night's deep azure dome
Darken'd the lawn and terrace high,
Where groups had left their music-room
For starry hush and open sky,
To watch the meteors, how they went
Across the stately firmament.

2.

As Walter paced with Josephine,
The loveliest maid of all he knew,
Touch'd by the vast and shadowy scene,
Their friendly spirits closer drew,
Beneath the dim-lit hollow night,
And those strange signals moving bright.

3.

" A wish," said Walter,—" have you heard—
  Wish'd in the shooting of a star,
Fulfils itself?" " Prepare your word,"
  Said Josephine; " there's nought to mar
The shining chance." " And may I tell?"
" O no! for that would break the spell."

4.

But now a splendid meteor flew,
  And ere it died the wish was made,
And won: for in a flash they knew
  The happy truth, so long delay'd,
Which months and years had never brought,
From this bright fleeting moment caught.

VII.

ON the Longest Day.
Heav'n was gay,
Roses and sunshine along the way.
I loiter'd and stood,
In listless mood,
With many a sigh,
I knew not why:
Nothing pleasant: nothing good.

On the Shortest Day,
Heav'n was grey,
Coldness and mire along the way.
How or where
Had I cast off care?

For light and strong,
With a snatch of song,
I stept through the mud and biting air.

Moods, that drift,
Or creep and shift,
Or change, not a windy cloud more swift,
No fetter found
To hold you bound,—
Can I dare to go
To the depth below
Whence ye rise, overspreading air and ground?

There in the gulf
Of my deep deep self,
Stranger than land of dragon and elf.
Acts and schemes,
Hopes and dreams,
Loves and praises,
Follies, disgraces,
Swarm, and each moment therewith teems.

They rise like breath
Of coming death,
Of flow'rs that the soul remembereth,

The Present, whose place
Is a footsole-space,
Being then as nought.
But the Present hath wrought
All this; and our Will is king, by God's grace.

38

VIII.

ABBEY ASAROE.

1.

GREY, grey is Abbey Asaroe, by Ballyshannon
town,
It has neither door nor window, the walls are broken
down;
The carven stones lie scatter'd in briar and nettle-bed.
The only feet are those that come at burial of the
dead.
A little rocky rivulet runs murmuring to the tide,
Singing a song of ancient days, in sorrow, not in
pride;
The bore-tree and the lightsome ash across the
portal grow,
And heaven itself is now the roof of Abbey Asaroe.

* "Bore-tree," a name for the elder-tree, *sambucus nigra*

2.

It looks beyond the harbour-stream to Bulban
  mountain blue;
It hears the voice of Erna's fall,—Atlantic breakers
  too;
High ships go sailing past it; the sturdy clank of
  oars
Brings in the salmon-boat to haul a net upon the
  shores;
And this way to his home-creek, when the summer
  day is done,
The weary fisher sculls his punt across the setting
  sun;
While green with corn is Sheegus Hill, his cottage
  white below;
But grey at every season is Abbey Asaroe.

3.

There stood one day a poor old man above its broken
  bridge:
He heard no running rivulet, he saw no mountain-
  ridge;
He turn'd his back on Sheegus Hill, and view'd
  with misty sight

The abbey walls, the burial-ground with crosses
   ghostly white;
Under a weary weight of years he bow'd upon his
   staff,
Perusing in the present time the former's epitaph;
For, grey and wasted like the walls, a figure full of
   woe,
This man was of the blood of them who founded
   Asaroe.

4.

From Derry Gates to Drowas Tower, Tirconnell
   broad was theirs;
Spearmen and plunder, bards and wine, and holy
   abbot's prayers;
With chanting always in the house which they had
   builded high
To God and to Saint Bernard,—whereto they came
   to die.
At worst, no workhouse grave for him! the ruins
   of his race
Shall rest among the ruin'd stones of this their
   saintly place.

The fond old man was weeping; and tremulous and
    slow
Along the rough and crooked lane he crept from
    Asaroe.

[Asaroe, *Eas-Aedha-Ruaidh*, Cataract of Red Hugh, a famous
    waterfall on the river Erne, where King Hugh is said to
    have been drowned about 2300 years ago, gave name to the
    neighbouring Abbey, founded in the twelfth century.]

IX

LATE AUTUMN.

O CTOBER,—and the skies are cool and grey
    O'er stubbles emptied of their latest sheaf.
Bare meadow, and the slowly falling leaf.
The dignity of woods in rich decay
Accords full well with this majestic grief
That clothes our solemn purple hills to-day,
Whose afternoon is hush'd, and wintry brief.
Only a robin sings from any spray,
And night sends up her pale cold moon, and spills
White mist around the hollows of the hills,
Phantoms of firth or lake: the peasant sees
His cot and stackyard, with the homestead trees,
In-islanded; but no vain terror thrills
His perfect harvesting; he sleeps at ease.

X.

ROBIN REDBREAST.

(A CHILD'S SONG.)

1.

GOODBYE, goodbye to Summer!
  For Summer's nearly done;
The garden smiling faintly,
  Cool breezes in the sun;
Our thrushes now are silent,
  Our swallows flown away,—
But Robin's here, in coat of brown,
  With ruddy breast-knot gay.
Robin, Robin Redbreast,
  O Robin dear!
Robin sings so sweetly
  In the falling of the year.

2.

Bright yellow, red, and orange,
  The leaves come down in hosts;

The trees are Indian Princes,
  But soon they'll turn to Ghosts;
The leathery pears and apples
  Hang russet on the bough;
Its Autumn, Autumn, Autumn late,
  'Twill soon be Winter now.
Robin, Robin Redbreast,
  O Robin dear!
And what will this poor Robin do?
  For pinching days are near.

3.

The fireside for the cricket,
  The wheatstack for the mouse.
When trembling night-winds whistle
  And moan all round the house;
The frosty ways like iron,
  The branches plumed with snow,—
Alas! in Winter dead and dark
  Where can poor Robin go?
Robin, Robin Redbreast,
  O Robin dear!
And a crumb of bread for Robin,
  His little heart to cheer.

XI.

SIR HUGH DE LA POLE.

1.

SIR HUGH DE LA POLE was a sturdy old
    knight,
Who in war and in peace had done every man right;
Had lived with his neighbours in loving accord,
Save the Abbot and Monks, whom he fiercely ab-
    horr'd,
And to their feet alone refused oak-floor and sward.

2.

With guests round his table, good servants at call,
His laughter made echo the wide castle-hall;
He whoop'd to the falcon, he hunted the deer;
If down by the Abbey, his comrades could hear—
" A plague on these mummers, who mime all the
    year!"

3.

And now see him stretch'd on his leave-taking bed.
Five minutes ago with a calm smile he said,
" I can trust my poor soul to the Lord God of
          Heaven,
" Though living unpriested and dying unshriven.
" Say all of you, friends, ' May his sins be forgiven!'"

4.

But some who are near to him sorely repine
He thus should decease like an ox or a swine:
So a message in haste to the Abbey they send,
When the voice cannot ring, and the arm cannot
          bend ;
For this reign, as all reigns do, approaches an end.

5.

Says my lady, " Too long I have yielded my mind."
Son Richard " to go with the world" is inclined.
" Sweet Mother of Mercy!" sobs Jane, his young
          spouse,
" O Saviour, forget not my tears and my vows!"
In pray'r for the dying her spirit she bows.

6.

At once the good Abbot forgets every wrong.
And speeds to the gate which repell'd him so long;
The stair (" Pax vobiscum!") is strange to his tread;
He puts everyone forth. Not a sound from that bed ;
And the spark from beneath the white eyebrow is
    fled.

7.

Again the door opens, all enter the place,
Where pallid and stern lies the well-beloved face.
" The Church, through God's help and Saint
    Simon's, hath won
To her bosom of pity a penitent son."
See the cross on his breast; hark, the knell is begun.

8.

Who feasts with young Richard? who shrives the
    fair Jane?
Whose mule to the Castle jogs right, without rein?
Our Abbey has moorland and meadowland wide,
Where Hugh for his hunting and hawking would
    ride,
Full of priest-hating whimsies and paganish pride.

9.

In the chancel the tomb is of Hugh de la Pole.
Ten thousand fine masses were said for his soul,
With praying, and tinkling, and incense, and flame:
In the centre whereof, without start or exclaim,
His bones fell to dust. You may still read the name,
'Twixt an abbot's and bishop's who once were of
        fame.

XII.

SONG.

O SPIRIT of the Summertime!
  Bring back the roses to the dells;
The swallow from her distant clime,
  The honey-bee from drowsy cells.

Bring back the friendship of the sun;
  The gilded evenings, calm and late,
When merry children homeward run,
  And peeping stars bid lovers wait.

Bring back the singing; and the scent
  Of meadowlands at dewy prime;—
Oh, bring again my heart's content,
  Thou Spirit of the Summertime!

XIII.

IN WEIMAR.

(OCTOBER, 1859.)

1.

IN little German Weimar,
  With soft green hills enfolded,
Where shady Ilm-brook wanders.
  A Great Man lived and wrote :
In life and art and nature
He conn'd their " open secret."
Of men and hours and fortunes
  He reverently took note.
Upon a verge of Europe,
Facing the silent sunsets,
And loud Atlantic billows.
  For me, too, rose his thought.
    Turn'd to a shape of stars on high
    Within the spiritual sky
    Of many an upward-gazing eye.

And now, this new October,
Within a holy garden,
'Mid flowers and trees and crosses,
   When dusk begins to fall,—
Where linden leaves are paling,
And poplar leaves are gilded,
And crimson is the wild-vine
   That hangs across the wall,—
I see the little temple
Wherein, with dust of princes,
The body lies of Goethe,
   And may not move at all.
      He mark'd all changes of the year:
      He loved to live; he did not fear
      The never-broken silence here.

Slow foots the grey old Sexton,
The ducal town's Dead-watcher.
Attending day and night time
   A bell that never rings;
The corpse upon the pallet,
A thread to every finger,—
The slightest touch would sound it,
   But silence broods and clings.

Beside the room of stillness,
While yet his couch is warmer,
This old man hath his biding,
   Therefrom the key he brings.
      For mighty mortals, in his day,
      He hath unlock'd the House of Clay,—
      For *them*, as we are wont to say.

By yellow-leafy midwalk
Slow foots that aged Sexton:
" *Ja wohl!* I have seen Goethe,
   And spoken too with him."
The lamp with cord he lowers,
And I, by steps descending,
Behold through grated doorway
   A chamber chill and dim,—
Gaze on a dark red coffer:
Full fourscore years were counted.
When that grand head lay useless,
   And each heroic limb.
      Schiller's dust is close beside,
      And Carl August's not far, denied
      His chosen place by princely pride.

The day had gloom'd and drizzled,
But clear'd itself in parting,
The hills were soft and hazy,
    Fine colours streak'd the west,
(Above that distant ocean)
And Weimar stood before me,
A dream of half my lifetime,
    A vision for the rest:
The House that fronts the fountain,
The Cottage at the woodside,—
Long since I surely knew them,
    But still, to see was best.

        Town and Park for eyes and feet:
        But all th' inhabitants I greet
        Are Ghosts, in every walk and street.

XIV.

EVERY DAY.

L ET us not teach and preach so much,
      But cherish, rather than profess;
Be careful how the thoughts we touch
      Of God, and Love, and Holiness,—

A charm, most spiritual. faint,
      And delicate. forsakes the breast,
Bird-like, when it perceives the taint
      Of prying breath upon its nest.

Using, enjoying, let us live:
      Set here to grow, what should we do
But take what soil and climate give?
      For thence must come our sap and hue:

Blooming as sweetly as we may,
      Nor beckon comers, nor debar:
Let them take balm or gall away,
      According as their natures are:

Look straight at all things from the soul,
    But boast not much to understand ;
Make each new action sound and whole,
    Then leave it in its place unscann'd :

Be true, devoid of aim or care ;
    Nor posture, nor antagonise :
Know well that clouds of this our air
    But seem to wrap the mighty skies :

Search starry mysteries overhead,
    Where wonders gleam ; yet bear in mind
That Earth 's our planet, firm to tread,
    Nor in the star-dance left behind :

For nothing is withheld, be sure,
    Our being needed to have shown ;
The far was meant to be obscure,
    The near was placed so to be known.

Cast we no astrologic scheme
    To map the course we must pursue ;
But use the lights whene'er they beam,
    And every trusty landmark too.

The Future let us not permit
  To choke us in its shadow's clasp:
It cannot touch us, nor we it:
  The present moment's in our grasp.

Soul sever'd from the Truth is Sin:
  The dark and dizzy gulf is Doubt:
Truth never moves,—unmoved therein,
  Our road is straight and firm throughout.

This Road for ever doth abide,
  The universe, if fate so call,
May sink away on either side:
  But This and God at once shall fall.

XV.

THE LUPRACAUN, OR FAIRY SHOEMAKER.

(A RHYME FOR THE CHILDREN.)

1.

LITTLE Cowboy, what have you heard,
Up on the lonely rath's green mound?
Only the plaintive yellow bird
Sighing in sultry fields around,
Chary, chary, chary, chee-ee!
Only the grasshopper and the bee?
   "Tip-tap, rip-rap,
    Tick-a-tack-too!
  Scarlet leather sewn together,
   This will make a shoe.
  Left, right, pull it tight:
   Summer days are warm;
  Underground in winter,
   Laughing at the storm!"

"Rath," ancient earthen fort.
"Yellow bird," the yellow-bunting, or *yorlin*.

Lay your ear close to the hill.

Do you not catch the tiny clamour—

Busy click of an elfin hammer,

Voice of the Lupracaun singing shrill

  As he merrily plies his trade?

    He's a span

    And a quarter in height.

Get him in sight, hold him tight,

    And you 're a made

      Man!

2.

You watch your cattle the summer day,

Sup on potatoes, sleep in the hay:

  How would you like to roll in your carriage,

  Look for a duchess's daughter in marriage?

Seize the Shoemaker—then you may!

  " Big boots a-hunting,

    Sandals in the hall,

  White for a wedding-feast,

    Pink for a ball.

  This way, that way,

    So we make a shoe:

Getting rich every stitch,
    Tick-tack-too !"
Nine-and-ninety treasure-crocks
This keen miser-fairy hath,
Hid in mountains, woods, and rocks,
Ruin and round-tow'r, cave and rath,
  And where the cormorants build ;
    From times of old
    Guarded by him ;
    Each of them fill'd
    Full to the brim
      With gold !

3.

I caught him at work one day, myself,
  In the castle-ditch where foxglove grows,—
A wrinkled, wizen'd, and bearded elf,
  Spectacles stuck on his pointed nose,
  Silver buckles to his hose,
  Leather apron—shoe in his lap—
    " Rip-rap, tip-tap,
      Tack-tack-too !
    (A grig skipp'd upon my cap,
      Away the moth flew)

Buskins for a fairy prince,
Brogues for his son, --
Pay me well, pay me well,
When the job is done!"
The rogue was mine, beyond a doubt.
I stared at him; he stared at me;
" Servant, Sir!" " Humph!" says he.
And pull'd a snuff-box out.
He took a long pinch, look'd better pleased.
The queer little Lupracaun;
Offer'd the box with a whimsical grace,—
Pouf! he flung the dust in my face,
And, while I sneezed,
Was gone!

XVI.

AFTER SUNSET.

THE vast and solemn company of clouds
    Around the Sun's death, lit, incarnadined,
Cool into ashy wan; as Night enshrouds
The level pasture, creeping up behind
Through voiceless vales, o'er lawn and purpled hill
And hazèd mead, her mystery to fulfil.
Cows low from far-off farms; the loitering wind
Sighs in the hedge, you hear it if you will,—
Though all the wood, alive atop with wings
Lifting and sinking through the leafy nooks,
Seethes with the clamour of ten thousand rooks.
Now every sound at length is hush'd away.
These few are sacred moments. One more Day
Drops in the shadowy gulf of bygone things.

XVII.

SOUTHWELL PARK.

I.—FROM THE HIGHWAY.

" FRIEND Edward, from this turn remark
  A vista of the Bridegroom's Park,
Fair Southwell, shut while you were here
By selfish Cupid, who allows
A sunny glimpse through beechen boughs
Of dells of grass with fallow deer,
And one white corner of the house
Built for the young Heir's wedding-day,
The dull old walls being swept away.
Wide and low, its eaves are laid
Over a slender colonnade,
Partly hiding, partly seen,
Amid redundant veils of green,
Which garland pillars into bowers,
And top them with a frieze of flowers:

The slight fence of a crystal door
(Like air enslaved by magic lore)
Or window reaching to the floor,
Divides the richly furnish'd rooms
From terraces of emerald sward,
Vases full of scarlet blooms,
And little gates of rose, to guard
The sidelong steps of easy flight;
Or, with a touch, they all unite.
All's perfect for a Bride's delight,
And She a worthy queen of all;
Gold-hair'd (I've seen her), slim and tall;
With---O a true celestial face
Of tender gravity and grace,
And gentle eyes that look you through,
Eyes of softly solemn blue.
Serene the wealthy mortal's fate,
Whose last wild-oats is duly sown!
Observe his Paradise's gate,
With two heraldic brutes in stone
For sentries.
        Did the coppice move?
A straggling deer perhaps.   By Jove!
A woman brushing through : she's gone.

Now what the deuce can bring her there?
Jog, lad: it's none of our affair.

 Well—you're to voyage, and I'm to stay.
Will Lucy kiss you, some other day,
When you carry your nuggets back this way?
You must not grow so rich and wise
That friends shall fail to recognise
The schoolboy-twinkle in your eyes.
Each his own track. I'll mind my farm,
And keep the old folk's chimney warm.
But however we strive, and chance to thrive,
We shall scarcely overtake this Youth,
Who has all to his wish, and seems in truth
The very luckiest man alive."

II.—BY THE POND.

" These walls of green, my Emmeline,
A labyrinth of shade and sheen,
Bar out the world a thousand miles,
Helping the pathway's winding wiles
To pose you to the end. Now think,
What thanks might one deserve for this—
Which lately was a swamp, and is

An elfin lake, its curving brink
Embost with rhododendron bloom,
Azaleas, lilies,—jewelries,
(Ruby and amethyst grow like these
Under our feet) on fire to dress,
Round every little glassy bay,
The sloping turf with gorgeousness?
As right, we look our best to day;
No petal dropt, no speck of gloom.

  Emmeline, this faery lake
Rose to its margins for your sake;
As yet without a name, it sues
Your best invention; think and choose.
Its flood is gather'd on the fells,
(Whose foldings you and I shall trace)
Hid in many a hollow place;
But through Himalayan dells,
Where the silvery pinnacles
Hanging faint in furthest heaven
Catch the flames of morn and even,
Round the lowest rampart swells
The surge of rhododendron flow'rs,
Indian ancestry of ours:
And the tropic woods luxuriantly

By Oronooko's river-sea
Nurtured the germs of this and this:
And there's a blossom first was seen
In a dragon-vase of white and green
By the sweetheart of a mandarin,
Winking her little eyes for bliss.

   Look, how these merry insects go
In rippling meshes to and fro,
Waltzing over the liquid glass,
Dropping their shadows to cross and travel,
Like ghosts, on the pavement of sunny gravel,
Maybe to music, whose thrills outpass
Our finest ear,—yes, even yours,
Whom the mysticism of sound allures
From star to star.   In this gulf beyond,
Silent people of the pond
Slip from noonday glare, to win
Their crystal twilights far within.
See the creatures glance and hide,
Turn, and waver, and glimmer, and glide,
Jerk away, ascend, and poise,
Come and vanish without noise,
Mope, with mouth of drowsy drinking,
Waving fins and eyes unwinking.

Flirt a tail, and shoot below.
How little of their life we know!
Or these birds' life that twittering dart
To the shrubbery's woven heart.
Which is happier, bird or fish?
Have they memory, hope, and wish?
Various temper? perverse will?
The secret source of boundless ill.
Why should not human creatures run
A careless course through shadow and sun?
Ah, Love, that may never be!
We are of a different birth,
Of deeper sphere than the fishes' home,
Higher than bird's wings may roam,
Greater than ocean, air, and earth.

 The Summer's youth is now at prime.
Swiftly a season whirls away.
Two days past, the bladed corn
Whisper'd nothing of harvest-time:
Already a tinge of brown is born
On the barley-spears that lightly sway:
The plumes of purple-seeded grass,
Bowing and bending as you pass,
Our mowers at the break of day

Shall sweep them into swathes of hay.

So the season whirls away.

And every aspect we must learn,

Southwell's every mood discern;

All sides, over the country speed.

' She upon her milk-white steed,

And he upon his grey,' to roam

Gladly, turn more gladly home;

Plan, improve, and see our tenants;

Visit neighbours, for pleasure or penance;

Excellent people some, no doubt,

And the rest will do to talk about.

June, July, and August: next

September comes; and here we stand

To watch those swallows, some clear day,

With a birdish trouble, half perplex'd,

Bidding adieu in their tribe's old way,

Though the sunbeam coaxes them yet to stay:

Swinging through the populous air,

Dipping, every bird, in play,

To kiss its flying image there.

And when Autumn's wealthy heavy hand

Paints with brown gold the beechen leaves.

And the wind comes cool, and the latest sheaves.

Quivers fill'd with bounty, rest
On stubble-slope,—then *we* shall say
Adieu for a time, our fading bow'rs,
Pictures within and out-of-doors,
And all the petted greenhouse flow'rs.
But, though your harp remains behind,
To keep the piano company,
Your gentle Spirit of Serenades
Shall watch with us how daylight fades
Where sea and air enhance their dyes
A thousand-fold for lovers' eyes.
And we shall fancy on far-off coast
The chill pavilions of the frost,
And landscapes in a snow-wreath lost.
—You, the well-fended nunlike child,
I, the bold youth, left loose and wild,
Join'd together for evermore,
To wander at will by sea and shore,—
Strange and very strange it seems!
More like the shifting world of dreams.

Choose a path, my Emmeline,
Through this labyrinth of green,
As though 'twere life's perplexing scene.
To go in search of your missing book,

You careless girl? one other search?
Wood or garden, which do you say?
'Twere only toil in vain: for, look—
I found it, free of spot or smirch,
On a pillow of wood-sorrel sleeping
Under the Fox's Cliff to-day.
Not so much as your place is lost,
Given to this delicate warden's keeping,—
Jasmin, that deserves to stay
Enshrined there henceforth, never toss'd
Like other dying blooms away.

   Summer, autumn, winter,—yes,
And much will come that we cannot guess:
Every minute brings its chance.

   Bend we now a parting glance
Down through the peaceful purity,
The shadow and the mystery,
As old saints look into their grave.
Water-elves may peep at me;
Only my own wife's face I see,
Like sunny light within the wave.
Dearer to me than sunny light.
It rose, and look'd away my night:

Whose phantoms, of desire or dread,
Like fogs and shades and dreams are fled."

III.—THROUGH THE WOOD.

" A fire keeps burning in this breast.
The smoke ascending to my brain
Sometimes stupefies the pain.
Sometimes my senses drop, no doubt.
I do not always feel the pain :
But my head is a weary weary load.

    What place is this ?—I sit at rest,
With grass and bushes round about ;
No dust, no noise, no endless road,
No torturing light.   Stay, let me think,
Is this the place where I knelt to drink,
And all my hair broke loose and fell
And floated in the cold clear well
Hung with rock-weeds ? two children came
With pitchers, but they scream'd and ran ;
The woman stared, the cursèd man
Laugh'd,—no, no, this is not the same.
I now remember.   Dragging through

The thorny fence has torn my gown.
These boots are very nearly done.
What matter? so 's my journey too.

   Nearly done . . . A quiet spot!
Flowers touch my hand.   It's summer now.
What summer meant I had forgot;
Except that it was glaring hot
Through tedious days, and heavy hot
Through dreadful nights.
               This drooping bough
Is elm; the shadow lies below.
Gathering flowers, we used to creep
Along the hedgerows, where the sun
Came through like this; then, every one,
Find out some arbour close and cool,
To weave them in our rushy caps,—
Primroses, bluebells, such a heap.
The children do so still, perhaps.
Some, too, were quite tall girls.
                You fool!
Was it for this you made your way
To Southwell Park by night and day?
—A million times I used to say

These two words, lest they might be lost:
After a while, turn where I would
I heard them. . . . This is his domain;
Each tree is his, each blade of grass
Under my feet. How dare I pass,
A tatter'd vagrant, half insane,
Scarce fit to slink by the roadside,
These lordly bounds, where, with his Bride—
I tell you, kneeling on this sod,
He is, before the face of God,
My husband!

    I was innocent
The day I first set eyes on him,
Eyes that no tears had yet made dim,
Nor fever wild. The day he went,
(That day, O God of Heaven!) I found,
In the sick brain slow turning round,
Dreadful forebodings of my fate.
A week was not so long to wait:
Another pass'd,—and then a third.
My face grew thin—eyes fix'd—I heard
And started if a feather stirr'd.
Each night ' to-morrow!' heard me say,
Each morning ' he will come to-day.'

Who taps upon the chamber door?—
A letter—he will come no more.
Then stupor.   Then a horrid strife
Trampling my brain and soul and life,—
Hunting me out as with a knife
From home—from home—

      And I was young,
And happy.   May his heart be wrung
As mine is! learn that even I
Was something, and at least can die
Of such a wound.   In any case
He'll see the death that's in my face.
To die is still within the power
Of girls with neither rank nor dower.

 This is Southwell.   I am here.
The house lay that side as one came.
How sick and deadly tired I am!
Time has been lost: O this new fear,
That I may fall and never rise!
Clouds come and go within my eyes.
I'm hot and cold, my limbs all slack,
My swollen feet the same as dead:
A weight like lead draws down my head,

The boughs and brambles pull me back.

Stay : the wood opens to the hill.

A moment now. The house is near.

But one may view it closer still

From these thick laurels on the right.

. . . What is this ? Who come in sight ?

He, with his Bride. It sends new might

Through all my feeble body. Hush !

Which way ? which way ? which way ? that bush

Hides them—they 're coming—do they pause ?

He points, almost to me !—he draws

Her tow'rds him, and I know the smile

That's on his face—O heart of guile !

No, 'twas the selfish gaiety

And arrogance of wealth. I see

Your Bride is tall, and graceful too.

That arch of leaves invites you through.

I follow. Why should I be loth

To hurt her ? . . . Ha ! I 'll find them both.

Six words suffice to make her know.

Both, both shall hear—it must be so."

IV.—MOSSGROWN.

" Seven years gone, and we together
Ramble as before, old Ned!
Not a brown curl on your head
Soil'd with touch of time or weather.
Yet no wonder if you fear'd,
With that broad chest and bushy beard,
Lucy might scarce remember you.
My letters, had they painted true
The child grown woman?

       Here's **our** way.
Autumn is in its last decay;
The hills have misty solitude
And silence; dead leaves drop in the wood.
And free in Southwell Park we stray,
Where only the too-much freedom baulks.
These half-obliterated walks,
The tangling grass, the shrubberies choked
With briars, the runnel which has soak'd
Its lawn-foot to a marsh, between
The treacherous tufts of brighter green,
The garden, plann'd with costly care,
Now wilder'd as a maniac's hair;

The blinded mansion's constant gloom,
Winter and summer, night and day,
Save when the stealthy hours let fall
A sunbeam, or more pallid ray,
Creeping across the floor and wall
From solitary room to room,
To pry and vanish, like the rest,
Weary of a useless quest;
The sombre face of hill and grove,
The very clouds which seem to move
Sadly, be it swift or slow,—
How unlike this, you scarcely know,
Was Southwell Park seven years ago.

   Human Spirits, line by line,
Have left hereon their visible trace;
As may, methinks, to Eye Divine,
Human history, and each one's share,
Be closely written everywhere
Over the solid planet's face.

   A sour old Witch,—a surly Youth,
Her grandson,—three great dogs, uncouth
To strangers (I'm on terms with all),
Are household now. Sometimes, at fall
Of dusk, a Shape is said to move

Amid the drear entangled grove,
Or seems lamentingly to stand
Beside a pool that's close at hand.
Rare are the human steps that pass
On mossy walk or tufted grass.

    Let's force the brushwood barrier,
No path remaining. Here's a chair!
Once a cool delightful seat,
Now the warty toad's retreat,
Cushion'd with fungus, sprouting rank,
Smear'd with the lazy gluey dank.
No doubt the Ghost sits often there—
A Female Shadow with wide eyes
And dripping garments. This way lies
The pool, the little pleasure-lake,
Which cost a pretty sum to make.
Stoop for this bough, and see it now
A dismal solitary slough,
Scummy, weedy, ragged, rotten,
Shut in jail, forsook, forgotten.

    Most of the story you have heard:
The bower of bliss at length prepared
To the last blossom, line of gilding,
(Never such a dainty building)

One day, Bride and Bridegroom came;
The hills at dusk with merry flame
Crowning their welcome: they had June,
Grand weather—and a honeymoon !
Came, to go away too soon,
And never come again.

The Bride

Was in her old home when she died,
On a winter's day, in the time of snow,
(She never saw that year to an end),
And he has wander'd far and wide,
And look'd on many a distant hill,
But not on these he used to know,
Round his Park that wave and bend,
And people think he never will.

Who can probe a spirit's pain ?
Who tell that man's loss, or gain ?
How far he sinn'd, how far he loved,
How much by what befell was moved,
If there his real happiness
Began, or ended, who shall guess ?
Trivial the biographic scroll
Save as a history of the soul,
Perhaps whose mightiest events

Are dumb and secret incidents.
A man's true life and history
Is like the bottom of the sea,
Where mountains and huge valleys hide
Below the wrinkles of the tide,
Under the peaceful mirror, under
Billowy foam and tempest-thunder.

Rude is the flower-shrubs' overgrowth,
Dark frowns the clump of firs beyond.
At twilight one might well be loth
To linger here alone, and find
The story vivid in one's mind.
A Young Girl, gently bred and fair,
A widow's daughter, whom the Heir
Met somewhere westward on a time,
Came down to this secluded pond,
That's now a mat of weeds and slime,
One summer-day seven years ago,
Sunshine above and flowers below:
Neglect had driven her to despair;
And, poor thing, in her frenzied mood
Bursting upon their solitude,
She drown'd herself, before the face
Of Bride and Bridegroom.   Here's the place.

Now mark—that very summer day
You, Ned, and I look'd down this way,
And saw the girl herself—yes, we!
Skirting the coppice—that was She.
    Imagine (this at least is known)
The frantic creature's plunge; the bride
Swooning by her husband's side;
And him, alone, and not alone,
Turning aghast from each to each,
Shouting for help, but none in reach.
He sees the drowning woman sink,
Twice—thrice—then, headlong from the brink,
He drags her to the grass—too late.
There by his servants was he found,
Bewilder'd by the stroke of fate;
With two pale figures on the ground,
One in the chill of watery death,
One with long-drawn painful breath
Reviving.   Sudden was the blow,
Dreadful and deep the change.   We go
To find the house.
                    Suspicion pries
From wrinkled mouth and wrinkled eyes,
Deaf dame! Yet constant friends are we.

G

Or never should I grasp this key,
Or tread this broad and lonely stair
From underground, or let this glare
Of outdoor world insult the gloom
That lives in each forsaken room,
Through which the gammer daily creeps,
And all from dust and mildew keeps.
Few hands may slide this veil aside,
To show—a picture of the Bride.
Is she not gently dignified?
Her curving neck, how smooth and long:
Her eyes, they softly look you through:
To think of violets were to wrong
Their lucency of living blue.

    The new hope of that fair young wife,
The sacred and mysterious life
Which counts as yet no separate hours,
Yielding to sorrow's hurtful powers,
Quench'd its faint gleam before a morn:
And when her breathless babe was born,
Almost as still the mother lay,
Almost as dumb, day after day,
Till on the tirth she pass'd away :
And far too soon her marriage-bell

Must now begin to ring her knell.
Greybeard, and child, and village-lass,
Who stood to see her wedding pass—
No further stoops the hoary head,
The merry maid is still unwed,
The child is yet a child, no more,
Watching her hearse go by their door.
Her bridal wreath one summer gave,
The next, a garland for her grave.

    Close the shutter.   Bright and sharp
The ray falls on those shrouded things,—
A grand piano and a harp,
Where no one ever plays or sings.

    Him ?—he hardly can forget.
Still, life goes on ; he's a young man yet :
His road has many a turn to take.
He may fell this wood, fill up the lake,
Throw down the house (so should not I),
Or sell it to you, Ned, if you'll buy.
Or, perhaps, come thoughtfully back some day,
With humble heart, and head grown grey.

    Homeward now, as quick as you will :
These afternoons are short and chill.
There's my haggart, under the hill :

Through evening's fog the cornstacks rise
Like domes of a little Arab city
Girt by its wall, with a bunch of trees
At a corner—palms, for aught one sees.
Sister Lucy is there alone;
The good old father and mother gone;
And I'm not married—more is the pity!
Seem I old bachelor in your eyes?
—Well, Ned, after dinner to-night,
When the ruddy hearth gives just the light
We used to think best, you'll spread your sail
And carry us far, without wave or gale;
And we'll talk of the old years, and the new,
Of what we have done, and mean to do."

XVIII.

THE LITTLE DELL.

DOLEFUL was the land,
  Dull on every side,
Neither soft nor grand,
  Barren, bleak, and wide;
Nothing look'd with love;
  All was dingy brown;
The very skies above
  Seem'd to sulk and frown.

Plodding sick and sad,
  Weary day on day:
Searching, never glad,
  Many a miry way;
Poor existence lagg'd
  In this barren place:
While the seasons dragg'd
  Slowly o'er its face.

Spring, to sky and ground,
　　Came before I guess'd :
Then one day I found
　　A valley, like a nest !
Guarded with a spell
　　Sure it must have been—
This little fairy dell
　　Which I had never seen.

Open to the blue,
　　Green banks hemm'd it round ;
A rillet wander'd through
　　With a tinkling sound ;
Briars among the rocks
　　A tangled arbour made :
Primroses in flocks
　　Grew beneath their shade.

Merry birds a few,
　　Creatures wildly tame,
Perch'd and sung and flew :
　　Timid fieldmice came :

Beetles in the moss
  Journey'd here and there ;
Butterflies across
  Danced through sunlit air.

There I often redd,
  Sung alone, or dream'd ;
Blossoms overhead,
  Where the west wind stream'd ;
Small horizon-line,
  Smoothly lifted up,
Held this world of mine
  In a grassy cup.

The barren land to-day
  Hears my last adieu :
Not an hour I stay ;
  Earth is wide and new.
Yet, farewell, farewell !
  May the sun and show'rs
Bless that Little Dell
  Of safe and tranquil hours !

XIX.

A WIFE.

THE wife sat thoughtfully turning over
  A book inscribed with the school-girl's name;
A tear, one tear, fell hot on the cover
  So quickly closed when her husband came.

He came and he went away, it was nothing;
  With commonplace words upon either side;
But, just with the sound of the room-door shutting,
  A dreadful door in her soul stood wide.

Love she had read of in sweet romances,
  Love that could sorrow, but never fail;
Built her own palace of noble fancies,
  All the wide world like a fairy-tale.

Bleak and bitter and utterly doleful
  Spread to this woman her map of life:

Hour after hour she look'd in her soul, full
    Of deep dismay and turbulent strife.

Face in hands, she knelt on the carpet;
    The cloud was loosen'd, the storm-rain fell.
O! life has so much to wilder and warp it,
    One poor heart's day what poet could tell?

XX.

OLD MASTER GRUNSEY AND GOOD-MAN DODD.

STRATFORD-ON-AVON, A.D. 1597.

G.

GOD save you, Goodman Dodd,—a sight to
    see you!

D. Save you, good Master Grunsey. Sir, how
    be you?

G. Middlish, thank heav'n. Rare weather for
    the wheat.

D. Farms will be thirsty, after all this heat.

G. And so is we. Sit down on this here bench:
We'll drink a pot o'yale, mun. Hither, wench!

My service—ha! I'm well enough, i' fegs,
But for this plaguey rheum i' both my legs.
Whiles I can't hardly get about: O dear!

   D. Thou see'st, we don't get younger every
      year.

   G. Thou'rt a young fellow yet.

   D.   Well-nigh three-score.

   G. I be thy elder fifteen year and more.
Hast any news?

   D.   Not much.   New-Place is sold,
And Willy Shakespeare's bought it, so I'm told.

   G. What, little Willy Shakespeare bought the
      Place!
Lord bless us, how young folk gets on apace!
Sir Hugh's great house beside the grammar-
      school!—
This Shakespeare's (take my word upon't) no fool.
I minds him sin' he were so high's my knee:

A stirrin' little mischief chap was he;
One day I cotch'd him peltin' o' my geese
Below the church: " You let 'en swim in peace,
" Young dog!" I says, " or I shall fling thee in."
Will was on t'other bank, and did but grin,
And call out, " Sir, you come across to here!"

D. I knows old John this five and thirty year.
In old times many a cup he made me drink;
But Willy weren't aborn then, I don't think.
Or might a' been a babe on's mother's arm,
When I did cart 'en fleeces from our farm.
I went a coortin' then, in Avon-Lane,
And, tho' bit further, I was always fain
To bring my cart thereby, upon a chance
To catch some foolish little nod or glance,
Or " meet me, Mary, wont 'ee, Charlcote way,
" Or down at Clopton Bridge, next holiday!"—
Health, Master Grunsey.

G.   Thank'ee, friend. 'Tis hot.
We might do warse than call another pot.
Good Mistress Nan! Will Shakespeare, troth, I
        know;

A nimble curly-pate, and pretty too,
About the street; he grow'd an idle lad,
And like enough, 'twas thought, to turn out bad :
I don't just fairly know, but folk did say
He vex'd the Lucys, and so fleed away.

D. He's warth as much as Tanner Twigg to-
    day ;
And all by plays in Lunnon.

G.   Folk talks big :
Will Shakespeare warth as much as Tanner
    Twigg—
Tut tut ! Is Will a player-man by trade ?

D. O' course he is, o' course he is : and made
A woundy heap o'money too, and bought
A playhouse for himself like, out and out :
And makes up plays, beside, for 'en to act :
Tho' I can't tell thee rightly, for a fact,
If out o' books or his own head it be.
We've other work to think on, thee and me.
They say Will's doin' finely, howsomever.

G. Why, Dodd, the little chap was always
          clever.

I don't know nothing now o' such-like toys;
New fashions plenty, mun, sin' we were boys:
We used to ha' rare mummings, puppet-shows,
And Moralties,—they can't much better those.
The Death of Judas was a pretty thing,
" So-la! so-la!" the Divil used to sing.
But time goes on, for sure, and fashion alters.

D. Up at the Crown, last night, says young
          Jack Walters,
" Willy's a great man now!"

G.   A jolterhead!
What does it count for, when all's done and said?
Ah! who'll obey, I t Will say " Come" or " Go"?
Such-like as him don't reckon much, I trow.
Sir, they shall travel first, like thee and me,
See London, to find out what great men be.
Ay, marry, must they.   Saints! to see the Court
Take water down to Greenwich: there's fine sport!
Her Highness in her frills and puffs and posies,
Barons, and lords, and chamberlains, and earls,

So thick as midges round her,—look at such
An thou would'st talk of greatness! why, the
    touch
Is on their stewards and lackeys, Goodman Dodd,
Who'll hardly answer Shakespeare wi' a nod,
And let him come, doff'd cap and bended knee.
We knows a trifle, neighbour, thee and me.

D. We may, Sir. This here's grand old Strat-
    ford brew;
No better yale in Lunnon, search it through.
New-Place ben't no such bargain, when all's done:
'Twas dear, I knows it.

G.   Thou bought'st better, man.
At Hoggin Fields: all ain't alike in skill.

D. Thanks to the Lord above! I've not done
    ill.
No more has thee, friend Grunsey, in thy trade.

G. So-so. But here's young Will wi' money
    made.

And money saved; whereon I sets him down,
Say else who likes, a credit to the town;
Tho' some do shake their heads at player-folk.

D. A very civil man, to chat and joke;
I've ofttimes had a bit o' talk wi' Will.

G. How doth old Master Shakespeare!

D.   Bravely still.
And so doth madam too, the comely dame.

   G. And Willy's wife—what used to be her
      name?

   D. Why, Hathaway, fro' down by Shottery
      gate.
I don't think she's so much about o' late.
Their son, thou see'st, the only son they had,
Died last year, and she took on dreadful bad;
And so the father did awhile, I'm told.
This boy o' theirs was nine or ten year old.
  Willy himself may bide here now, mayhap.

G. He always was a clever little chap.

I'm glad o' his luck, an 'twere for old John's
    sake.

Your arm, sweet sir. Oh, how my legs do
    ache!

XXI.

THE POOR LITTLE MAIDEN.

1.

A GENTLE face and clear blue eyes
The little maiden hath, who plies
Her needle at the cottage door,
Or, with a comrade girl or more,
Group'd on the shady hedgerow-grass.
I love to find her as I pass,—
Humbly contented, simply gay,
And singing sweetly: many a day
I've carried far along my way
From that fair infant's look and voice
A strength that made my soul rejoice.

Oh! her father died last week;
Her mother knows not where to seek.

Five children's food; the little maid
Is far too young for others' aid.
Willingly would she do her best
To slave at strangers' rude behest;
But she is young and weak.   Her thread,
From dawn till blinding rushlight sped,
Could never win her single bread.

3.

And must the Poorhouse save alive
This Mother and her helpless five,
Where Guardians, no Angelic band,
With callous eye and pinching hand,
Receive the wretched of their kin,
Cursing the law that lets them in?
I see her growing pale and thin,
Poor Child; (the little needle-song
Is ended)—and perhaps ere long
Her coffin jolting in their cart
To where the paupers lie apart.

4.

ust from that cottage-step one sees
A Mansion with its lawn and trees.

Where man and wife are wearing old
Within a wilderness of gold,
Amidst all luxuries and graces,
Except the light of children's faces.
Ah, had the little Maid forlorn
In that fine house been only born,
How she were tended, night and morn!
A long-tail'd pony then were hers,
And winter mantles edged with furs,
And servants at her least command.
And wealthy suitors for her hand.

XXII.

SONG—" ACROSS THE SEA."

1.

I WALK'D in the lonesome evening,
  And who so sad as I,
When I saw the young men and maidens
  Merrily passing by.
    To thee, my Love, to thee—
    So fain would I come to thee!
While the ripples fold upon sands of gold
    And I look across the sea.

2.

  I stretch out my hands; who will clasp them?
  I call,—thou repliest no word:
O why should heart-longing be weaker
  Than the waving wings of a bird!

To thee, my Love, to thee—
So fain would I come to thee !
For the tide's at rest from east to west.
And I look across the sea.

3.

There's joy in the hopeful morning,
There's peace in the parting day,
There's sorrow with every lover
Whose true-love is far away.
To thee, my Love, to thee—
So fain would I come to thee !
And the water's bright in a still moonlight.
As I look across the sea.

XXIII.

HIS TOWN.

A FAR-OFF Town my memory haunts,
    Shut in by fields of corn and flax,
Like housings gay on elephants
    Heaved on the huge hill-backs.

How pleasantly that image came !
    As down the zigzag road I press'd,
Blithe, but unable yet to claim
    His roof from all the rest.

And I should see my Friend at home,
    Be in the little town at last
Those welcome letters dated from,
    Gladdening the two years past.

I recollect the summer-light,
   The bridge with poplars at its end,
The slow brook turning left and right,
   The greeting of my friend.

I found him; he was mine,—his books,
   His home, his day, his favourite walk,
The joy of swift-conceiving looks,
   The wealth of living talk.

July, no doubt, comes brightly still
   On blue-eyed flax and yellowing wheat;
But sorrow shadows vale and hill
   Since one heart ceased to beat.

Is not the climate colder there,
   Since that Youth died?—it must be so;
A dumb regret is in the air;
   The brook repines to flow.

Wing'd thither, fancy only sees
   An old church on its rising ground,
And underneath two sycamore trees
   A little grassy mound.

XXIV.

HYMN.

O HOW dimly walks the wisest
    On his journey to the grave,
Till Thou, Lamp of Souls, arisest,
    Beaming over land and wave !

Blind and weak behold him wander,
    Full of doubt and full of dread ;
Till the dark is rent asunder,
    And the gulf of light is spread.

Shadows were the gyves that bound him,
    Now his soul is light in light ;
Heav'n within him, Heav'n around him,
    Pure, eternal, infinite.

XXV.

THE QUEEN OF THE FOREST.

(A FANTASY.)

1.

BEAUTIFUL, beautiful Queen of the Forest,
How art thou hidden so wondrous deep?
Bird never sung there, fay never morriced,
All the trees are a-sleep.
Nigh the drizzling waterfall
Pluméd ferns wave and wither;
Voices from the woodlands call,
"Hither, O hither!"
Calling all the summer day,
Through the woodlands, far away.

2.

Who by the rivulet loiters and lingers,
Tranced by a mirror, a murmur, a freak;
Thrown where the grass's cool fine fingers
Play with his dreamful cheek?

Cautious creatures gliding by,
    Mystic sounds fill his pleasure,
Tangled roof inlaid with sky,
    Flowers, heaps of treasure :
Wandering slowly all the day,
Through the woodlands, far away.

3.

Late last night, betwixt moonlight and morning,
    Came She, unthought of, and stood by his bed ;—
A kiss for love, and a kiss for warning,
    A kiss for trouble and dread.
Now her flitting fading gleam
    Haunts the woodlands wide and lonely :
Now, a half-remember'd dream
    For his comrade only,
He shall stray the livelong day
Through the forest, far away.

4.

Dare not the hiding enchantress to follow :
    Hearken the yew, he hath secrets of hers.
The grey owl stirs in an oaktree's hollow,
    The wind in the gloomy firs.

Down among those dells of green,
    Glimpses, whispers, run to wile thee:
Waking eyes have nowhere seen
    Her that would beguile thee—
Draw thee on, till death of day,
Through the dusk woods, far away.

XXVI.

PROGRESS.

" GIVE back my youth!" the poets cry,
    " Give back my youth!"—so say not I.
Youth play'd its part with us; if we
Are losers, should we gainers be
By recommencing, with the same
Conditions, all the finish'd game?
If we see better now, we are
Already winners just so far,—
And merely ask to keep our winning,
Wipe out loss, for a new beginning!
This may come, in Heaven's good way,
How, no mortal man shall say:
But not by fresh-recover'd taste
For sugarplums, or valentines,
Or conjuring back the brightest day
Which gave its gift and therefore shines.

Win or lose, possess or miss,
There cannot be a weaker waste
Of memory's privilege than this—
To dwell among cast-off designs.
Stages, larvæ of yourself,
And leave the true thing on the shelf.
The Present-Future, wherewith blend
Hours that hasten to their end.

XXVII.

THE WINDING BANKS OF ERNE:

OR. THE EMIGRANT'S ADIEU TO

BALLYSHANNON.

(A LOCAL BALLAD.)

1.

ADIEU to Ballyshannon! where I was bred
and born:
Go where I may, I'll think of you, as sure as night
and morn,
The kindly spot, the friendly town, where every
one is known,
And not a face in all the place but partly seems my
own;
There's not a house or window, there's not a field
or hill,
But, east or west, in foreign lands, I'll recollect
them still.

I leave my warm heart with you, though my back
    I'm forced to turn—
So adieu to Ballyshannon, and the winding banks
    of Erne!

2.

No more on pleasant evenings we'll saunter down
    the Mall,
When the trout is rising to the fly, the salmon to
    the fall.
The boat comes straining on her net, and heavily
    she creeps,
Cast off, cast off!—she feels the oars, and to her
    berth she sweeps:
New fore and aft keep hauling, and gathering up
    the clue,
Till a silver wave of salmon rolls in among the crew.
Then they may sit, with pipes a-lit, and many a joke
    and 'yarn':—
Adieu to Ballyshannon, and the winding banks
    of Erne!

3.

The music of the waterfall, the mirror of the tide,
When all the green-hill'd harbour is full from side
    to side—

From Portnasun to Bulliebawns, and round the
   Abbey Bay,
From rocky Inis Saimer to Coolnargit sandhills
   grey;
While far upon the southern line, to guard it like
   a wall,
The Leitrim mountains, clothed in blue, gaze calmly
   over all,
And watch the ship sail up or down, the red flag
   at her stern :—
Adieu to these, adieu to all the winding banks of
   Erne !

4.

Farewell to you, Kildoney lads, and them that
   pull an oar,
A lug-sail set, or haul a net, from the Point to
   Mullaghmore :
From Killybegs to bold Slieve-League, that ocean-
   mountain steep,
Six hundred yards in air aloft, six hundred in the
   deep :
From Dooran to the Fairy Bridge, and round by
   Tullan strand.

Level and long, and white with waves, where gull
and curlew stand;—
Head out to sea when on your lee the breakers
you discern !—
Adieu to all the billowy coast, and winding banks
of Erne !

5.

Farewell Coolmore,—Bundoran! and your summer
crowds that run
From inland homes to see with joy th' Atlantic-
setting sun;
To breathe the buoyant salted air, and sport among
the waves;
To gather shells on sandy beach, and tempt the
gloomy caves;
To watch the flowing, ebbing tide, the boats, the
crabs, the fish;
Young men and maids to meet and smile, and form
a tender wish;
The sick and old in search of health, for all things
have their turn—
And I must quit my native shore, and the winding
banks of Erne !

6.

Farewell to every white cascade from the Harbour
   to Belleek,
And every pool where fins may rest, and ivy-shaded
   creek;
The sloping fields, the lofty rocks, where ash and
   holly grow,
The one split yew-tree gazing on the curving
   flood below;
The Lough, that winds through islands under
   Turaw mountain green;
And Castle Caldwell's stretching woods, with
   tranquil bays between;
And Breesie Hill, and many a pond among the
   heath and fern,—
For I must say adieu—adieu to the winding banks
   of Erne!

7.

The thrush will call through Camlin groves the
   livelong summer day;
The waters run by mossy cliff, and bank with wild
   flowers gay;
The girls will bring their work and sing beneath
   a twisted thorn,

Or stray with sweethearts down the path among
the growing corn;

Along the river side they go, where I have often
been,—

O, never shall I see again the days that I have seen!

A thousand chances are to one I never may
return,—

Adieu to Ballyshannon, and the winding banks
of Erne!

8.

Adieu to evening dances, when merry neighbours
meet,

And the fiddle says to boys and girls, "Get up and
shake your feet!"

To "shanachus" and wise old talk of Erin's days
gone by—

Who trench'd the rath on such a hill, and where
such king might lie

Or ...... of king, or warrior chief; with tales of
fairy power,

And tender ditties sweetly sung to pass the twilight
hour.

The mournful song of exile is now for me to
learn—

Adieu, my dear companions on the winding banks
of Erne!

9.

Now measure from the Commons down to each
end of the Purt,

Round the Abbey, Moy, and Knather,—I wish no
one any hurt;

The Main Street, Back Street, College Lane, the
Mall, and Portnasun,

If any foes of mine are there, I pardon every
one.

I hope that man and womankind will do the same
by me;

For my heart is sore and heavy at voyaging the
sea.

My loving friends I'll bear in mind, and often
fondly turn

To think of Ballyshannon, and the winding banks
of Erne.

10.

If ever I'm a money'd man, I mean, please God,
to cast

My golden anchor in the place where youthful
years were pass'd;

Though heads that now are black and brown must
meanwhile gather grey,

New faces rise by every hearth, and old ones drop
away—

Yet dearer still that Irish hill than all the world
beside;

It's home, sweet home, where'er I roam, through
lands and waters wide.

And if the Lord allows me, I surely will return

To my native Ballyshannon, and the winding
banks of Erne.

XXVIII.

LOSS.

GRIEVE not much for loss of wealth,
   Loss of friends, or loss of fame,
Loss of years, or loss of health;
   Answer, hast thou lost the shame
Whose early tremor once could flush
Thy cheek, and make thine eyes to gush,
And send thy spirit, sad and sore,
To kneel with face upon the floor,
Burden'd with consciousness of sin?
Art thou cold and hard within,—
Sometimes looking back surprised
On thy old mood, scarce recognized,
As on a picture of thy face
In blooming childhood's transient grace?
Then hast thou cause for grief; and most
In seldom missing what is lost.

With the loss of Yesterday,
　　Thou hast lost To-day, To-morrow,--
All thou might'st have been.　O pray,
　　(If pray thou canst) for poignant sorrow!

XXIX.

WINTER VERDURE.

I SAT at home, and thought there lived no
    green,
Because the time is winter; but, to-day,
Entering a park a mile or two away,
Smooth laurels tower'd as if no cold had been:
The tangled ivy, holly sharp and sheen,
Hung over nested ferns, and craglets grey
Broider'd with moss; high firs, a drooping screen,
Guarded their turfy lawn in close array.
Soon shall the hopeful woodbine-garland swing,
And countless buds the misty branch impearl:
My little Portress, fair come Spring to you,
Life's and the year's, flow'r-cheek'd and sparkling
    girl!
Or are you, child, the Spirit of the Spring,
Safe in these warmer groves the winter through?

XXX.

A DREAM OF A GATE.

"THE LETTER KILLETH, BUT THE SPIRIT GIVETH LIFE."

1.

RESPECT thine office; fear no man;
Thou, Poet, art a sacristan,
(For higher creatures than poor we,
I think, are priests invisibly)
'Tis thine to tread on holy ground,
Where meaner foot is wrongly found;
'Tis thine to guard the Mysteries,—
Which are not shown to mortal eyes
The purest, clearest,—from disgrace
Of idols in the sacred place.

2.

By names of Venus and of Mars
The Tuscan Exile fill'd the stars
With lover and with warrior souls:
Aloof each mighty planet rolls,

By sagest Poet unconceived.
Fancy on fancy, half-believed,
Forget how they have sprung from nought.
I often pictured in my thought
A Gate, whereof we speak and write ;
And found the same at dead of night,
Neither by moon nor lantern-light.

3.

It was, in dreaming truth, a Gate
Vaster than kings go through in state,
And pierced a black gigantic wall
Immeasurably built.   To all,
Wide, without bar or valve, it stood.
And round it throng'd a Multitude,
From every nation that has birth
Between the snowy poles of Earth.

4.

As bursts the sunshine from a cave
Of high cloud, over field and wave,
One, like a man, but more than mortal,
Radiantly issues from the Portal,—
Realm within it softly bright,
Purple shadow and golden light,

On mystic mountains, happy vales,
Where circle beyond circle fails.

5.

" Come in !"—'twas music trumpet-clear.
" The Gate of Heaven is open here."
Whereat, a wind of joy and fear
Swept all that mighty Multitude,
All one way leaning, all subdued
To silence, save a whispering stress
Born from the hush of earnestness.

6.

But jangling tones broke up the charm,
As bells a sleeping town alarm :
" Beloved Sheep, beware, beware !
" This is no true thing, but a snare :
" No note or mark or sign or token
" Whereof the oracles have spoken.
" This like our promised Heaven ! so mix
" With heathens and with ——— !
" Apollyon ——— Son of Light.
" But soon the Bridegroom shall invite,

" We're saved, the others flung to Hell,
" And hallelujah! all is well.
" Close eye and ear, my brethren,—say
" Phantom! Delusion! Fiend! away!"

7.

Suddenly a little Child
Ran up to where that Angel smiled,
And caught his skirt; who, stooping low,
Lifted him; and I saw them go,
And sigh'd,—and sighing, waken'd so:
Amidst, methought, a boundless flow
Of people, many voices blent,
Sea-like; I knew not what it meant.

8.

Saint Wilbrod, where a Pagan King
Knelt at the font, had bow'd to fling
Miraculous water on his head:
But the grave King rose up, and said.
" This was not thought of: can'st thou tell
" If my forefathers be in Hell.
" Or Heaven?" " In Hell," the saint's reply.
To whom the King with loftier eye,

" Enough ! I will not quit my race."
—To answer, *Heaven is not a place,*
Were bringing passports to disgrace.

9.

Such doctrines Mather fear'd at Salem,*
And, lest his own belief should fail him,
(So godly, that he turn'd inhuman)
Hang'd twice a week some poor old woman,
Nay, Brother Burroughs' self, who doubted,—
That Scripture's letter be not scouted;
Which, with all marvels big and little,
Not held and hugg'd in every tittle,
Faith were slain dead (that 's now so strong),
And Truth, and Sense of Right and Wrong;
Yes, the ALMIGHTY then, no doubt,
From soul of man were blotted out.

10.

Predominancy, a great tree
Of Upas kind, drips constantly
The violent poison, Persecution;

* Read a curious and instructive record in Chapter XIX. of
Bancroft's *History of the United States.*

Greater the marvel, though, if you shun
Harm from a small infesting weed
Which doth the self-same venom breed,
Verbality, whose mesh is found
In every field and garden-ground.
Spirit to spirit, we are wise
To meditate of mysteries,
To see a little, dark and dim,
For mortals are not Seraphim.

11.

A Dream should as a dream be told,
Nor do I this of mine uphold
Above the dreams of other men,
Where all is out of waking ken.
Let's to our daylight tasks, and trust
The future, as we ought and must.
Go, noisy tongues, howe'er you will !
One hath His plan, who keepeth still.
What is, He sees,—we cannot see ;
He knows, we know not, what shall i.

12.

Though High-Priest, Medicine-man, nor Lan...,
Zerdusht, Mohammed, Buddh, nor Brahm...,

Nor any Prophet, meek or blatant,
For true Religion hold a patent,
Can mathematicise the line
Connecting Human and Divine,
The line, say rather, that doth reach
From God to every soul and each,—
Though Spurgeon's overhead revealing
Pierce not the tabernacle-ceiling,—
Th'Augur of Crown-Court might play
' Sensation' parts across the way,
With less affront to his own soul,
And yours, than in his present rôle,—
Though Pio Nono know no more
Than Cantuar. of Peter's Door,
Nor more than whoso made the last
... silly serious book that fast
Through ninety-five editions pass'd,—
Though every parable and vision
Of scenes infernal and elysian.
By prophet-poet's genius told,
... echo'd them a-million-fold,
... of Greek, or Jew, or Swede.
... really no more indeed
... any fairy-tale we read,—

Though man's best wisdom on the earth,
Man's learning, be as little worth
For this, as to be six feet one
Helps you to pry into the sun,--
Still, when the Soul is walking right,
HEAVEN is sure to come in sight,
Near or distant, faint or bright.

XXXI.

DANGER.

I STROVE for wicked peace, but might not win:
  The bonds would bite afresh, one moment
      slack.
" Then burst them !" . . . . instantly I felt begin
Damnation. Falling through a chasm of black,
I swiftly sunk thousands of miles therein.
Soul grew incorporate with gross weight of sin,
Death clung about my feet: let none dare track
My journey. But a far Voice call'd me back.
I breathe this world's infatuating air,
And tremble as I walk. Most men are bold—
Perchance through madness. O that I could hold
One path, nor wander to the fen, nor dare
Between the precipice and wild-beast's lair !
For penalties are stablish'd from of old.

XXXII.

THE ABBOT OF INNISFALLEN.

(A KILLARNEY LEGEND.)

1.

THE Abbot of Innisfallen
    Awoke ere dawn of day :
Under the dewy green leaves
    Went he forth to pray.

The lake around his island
    Lay smooth and dark and deep,
And wrapt in a misty stillness
    The mountains were all asleep.

Low kneel'd the Abbot Cormac.
    When the dawn was dim and grey :
The prayers of his holy office
    He faithfully 'gan say.

Low kneel'd the Abbot Cormac,
  When the dawn was waxing red;
And for his sins' forgiveness
  A solemn prayer he said:

Low kneel'd that holy Abbot,
  When the dawn was waxing clear;
And he pray'd with loving-kindness
  For his convent-brethren dear.

Low kneel'd that blessed Abbot,
  When the dawn was waxing bright;
He pray'd a great prayer for Ireland,
  He pray'd with all his might.

Low kneel'd that good old Father,
  While the sun began to dart:
He pray'd a prayer for all mankind,
  He pray'd it from his heart.

2.

The Abbot of Innisfallen
  Arose upon his feet:
He heard a small bird singing,
  And O but it sung sweet!

He heard a white bird singing well
  Within a holly-tree;
A song so sweet and happy
  Never before heard he.

It sung upon a hazel,
  It sung upon a thorn;
He had never heard such music
  Since the hour that he was born.

It sung upon a sycamore,
  It sung upon a briar;
To follow the song and hearken
  This Abbot could never tire.

Till at last he well bethought him;
  He might no longer stay;
So he bless'd the little white singing-bird,
  And gladly went his way.

3.

But, when he came to his Abbey-walls,
  He found a wondrous change;
He saw no friendly faces there,
  For every face was strange.

The strange men spoke unto him ;
    And he heard from all and each
The foreign tongue of the Sassenach,
    Not wholesome Irish speech.

Then the oldest monk came forward,
    In Irish tongue spake he :
" Thou wearest the holy Augustine's dress,
    And who hath given it to thee?"

" I wear the holy Augustine's dress,
    And Cormac is my name,
The Abbot of this good Abbey
    By grace of God I am.

" I went forth to pray, at break of day :
    And when my prayers were said,
I hearken'd awhile to a little bird,
    That sung above my head."

The monks to him made answer,
    " Two hundred years have gone o'er,
Since our Abbot Cormac went through the gate,
    And never was heard of more.

" Matthias now is our Abbot,
    And twenty have pass'd away.
The stranger is lord of Ireland;
    We live in an evil day."

4.

" Now give me absolution ;
    For my time is come," said he.
And they gave him absolution,
    As speedily as might be.

Then, close outside the window,
    The sweetest song they heard
That ever yet since the world began
    Was utter'd by any bird.

The monks look'd out and saw the bird,
    Its feathers all white and clean ;
And there in a moment, beside it,
    Another white bird was seen.

Those two they sang together,
    Waved their white wings, and fled :
Flew aloft, and vanish'd ;—
    But the good old man was dead.

They buried his blessed body
    Where lake and greensward meet:
A carven cross above his head,
    A holly-bush at his feet:

Where spreads the beautiful water
    To gay or cloudy skies,
And the purple peaks of Killarney
    From ancient woods arise.

XXXIII.

SUNDAY BELLS.

SWEET Sunday Bells! your measured sound
Enhances that repose profound
Of all the golden fields around,
And range of mountain, sunshine-drown'd.

Amid the cluster'd roofs outswells,
And wanders up the winding dells,
And near and far its message tells,
Your holy song, sweet Sunday Bells!

Sweet Sunday Bells! ye summon round
The youthful and the hoary-crown'd,
To one observance gravely bound;
Where comfort, strength, and joy are found.

The while, your cadenced voice excels
To waken memory's tender spells:

Revives old joy-bells, funeral-knells,
And childhood's far-off Sunday Bells.

O Sunday Bells! your pleading sound
The shady spring of tears hath found,
In one whom neither pew nor mound
May harbour in the hallow'd ground:

Whose heart to your old music swells;
Whose soul a deeper thought compels;
Who like an alien sadly dwells
Within your chime, sweet Sunday Bells!

XXXIV.

TWO FAIRIES IN A GARDEN.

"WHITHER goest, brother elf?"

" The sun is weak—to warm myself
In a thick red tulip's core.
Whither thou?"

" Till day be o'er,
To the dim and deep snow-palace
Of the closest lily-chalice,
Where is veil'd the light of noon
To be like my Lady's moon.
Thou art of the day, I ween?"

" Yet I not disown our Queen.
Nor at Lyse' am backward found
When the mighty feast comes round;

When She spreads abroad her power
To proclaim a midnight hour
For the pale blue fays like thee
And the ruddy elves like me
To mingle in a charmèd ring
With a perfect welcoming;
Guarded from the moon-stroke cold,
And wisp that scares us on the wold."

" Swift that Night is drawing near,
When your abrupt and jovial cheer
Mixes in our misty dance,
Meeting else by rarest chance.
We love dark undew'd recesses
Of the leafy wildernesses,
Or to hide in some cold flower
Shelter'd from the sunlight hour,
And more afflictive mortal eye."

" Gladly, gladly, do I spy
Human children playing nigh,
Feel, and so must you, the grace
Of a loving human face.
Else why come you in this place?

O my sister, if we might
Show ourselves to mortal sight
Far more often !—if they knew
Half the friendly turns we do !
Even now, a gentle thought
Pays our service dimly wrought.
The paler favourites of the moon
Cannot give nor take such boon !"

" Chantings, brother, hear you might,
Softly sung through still of night;
Calling from the wëird North
Dreams like distant echoes forth,
Till through curtain'd shades they creep.
To inlay the gloomy floor of sleep
For babes, and souls that babe-like are :
So we bless them from afar
Like a faint but favouring star.
 --But tell me how in fields or bowers
Thou hast spent these morning hours ?"

" Through the tall hedge I have been,
Shadowy wall of crusted green,
Within whose heart the birds are seen.

Speeding swiftly thence away
To the crowning chestnut-spray,
I watch'd a tyrant steal along
Would slay the sweet thrush in her song;
Warn'd, she soon broke off from singing,
There we left the branchlet swinging.
Whispering robin, down the walk,
News of poising, pouncing hawk,
The sycamore I next must strew
On every leaf with honey-dew.
And hither now from clouds I run;
For all my morning work is done."

" Alas, I wither in the sun,
Witless drawn to leave my nest
Ere the day be laid to rest!
But to-night we lightly troop
By the young moon's silver hoop:
Weaving wide our later ranks
As on evening river-banks
Shifting crowds of midges glance
Through mazes of their airy dance:
O might you come, O might you see
All our shadow'd revelry!

Yet the next night shall be rarer,
Next and next and next, still fairer;
We are waxing every night,
Till our joy be full and bright;
Then as slowly do we wane
With gentle loss that makes no pain.
For thus are we with life endued:
Ye, I trow, have rougher food."

" Yes: with fragrant soul we're fed
Of every flower whose cheek is red,
Shunning yellow, blue, and white;
And southward go, at the nightingale's flight.
Many the faery nations be.
O! how I long, I long to see
The moonèd midnight of our feast
Flushing amber through the east,
When every cap in Elfendom
Into that great ring shall come,
Owl and elf and fairy blended,
Till th' imperial time be ended!
Even those fantastic Sprites
Lay aside their dear delights
Of freakish mischief and annoyance

In the universal joyance,
One of whom I saw of late
As I peep'd through window-grate,
(Under roof I may not enter)
Haunt the housewife to torment her:
Tangle up her skeins of silk,
Throw a mouse into her milk,
Hide her thimble, scorch her roast,
Quickly drive her mad almost:
And I too vex'd, because I would
Have brought her succour if I could.
  —But where shall this be holden, say?
Far away?"

          " O, far away,
Over river must we fly,
Over the sea, and the mountain high,
Over city, seen afar
Like a low and misty star,—
Soon beneath us glittering
Like million spark-worms.   But our wing
For the flight will ne'er suffice.
Some are training flitter-mice,
I a silver moth."

" Be ware
How I'll thrid the vaulted air !
A dragon-fly with glassy wings,
Born beside the meadow springs,
That can arrow-swiftly glide
Thorough the glowing eventide,
Nor at twilight-fall grow slack,
Shall bear me on his long red back.
Dew-stars, meteors of the night,
May not strike him with affright,
He can needle through the wood,
That 's like a green earth-chainèd cloud,
Mountain-summits deftly rake ;
Draw swift line o'er plain and lake ;
If at Lyseo I be last,
Other elves must journey fast.
Lu a vo !"

" But Elf, I rede,
Of all your herbs take special heed.
Our Mistress tholes no garden flowers,
Though we have freedom of these bowers.
Tell me what you mean to treasure,
Each in 's atom ?"

L

" Gold-of-Pleasure,
Medic, Plumeseed, Fountain-arrow,
Vervain, Hungry-grass, and Yarrow,
Quatrefoil and Melilot."

" These are well. And I have got
Moonwort and the Filmy Fern,
Gather'd nicely on the turn.
Wo to fairy that shall bring
Bugloss for an offering,
Toad-flax, Barley of the Wall.
Enchanter's Nightshade, worst of all.
—Oh, brother, hush! I faint with fear!
A mortal foot-step threatens near."

" None can see us, none can hear.
Yet, to make thee less afraid.
Hush we both as thou hast pray'd.
I will seek the verse to spell
Written round my dark flow'r's bell,
To sing at sunset. Fare-thee-well!"

XXXV.

EMILY.

" **G**OOD evening.   Why, of course it's you !
You ' half-imagined,'—O I knew !
There, there, don't make a fuss, my dear,
Come in and let's have supper here.

You're married now, George ; yes, I heard :
And looking bright. upon my word.
And I !—a little thin or so ?—
One can't make cottage-roses grow
As well in London—O dear me !
But never mind ; its life, you see.

Her name—don't tell me ; I don't care.
Of course you make a loving pair.
Your jolly healths !   Why, there you sit,
And never eat or drink a bit.

' How well I'm drest'—you think so, eh ?
You like my hair done up this way ?

Oh don't go yet, George ! stay, do stay !
Five minutes longer ! please don't go !
I 'm not fit company, I know—
But just this one time—just this last !

D 'ye ever think of days gone past,
When you and I a-courting went,
So loving, and so innocent ?
Our walks, our little messages,
Our notes, our quarrels ; after these,
Our makings-up—O were we not
Rare fools ! Then, of a sudden, came
The desperate quarrel, and for what !
For nothing !—I was most to blame.

What use in crying ! Ain't it funny !
Nay, my good sir, I don't want money.
I don't, George : no, I don't indeed.
Why, I can lend you if you need.
Stop, I 'll take this : I 'll tell you why :
A little locket I shall buy.

(Now mayn't I ?) big enough to hold
A lock of hair, that you forgot,
And so I kept it back.

How cold
The night-air strikes when one's so hot!
Ah, you won't kiss me now.   All right.
Ta-ta, George; off you go; good-night!"

XXXVI.

NIGHTWIND.

MOANING blast,
　　The summer is past,
And time and life are speeding fast.

Wintry wind,
　　Oh, where to find
The hopes we have left so far behind!

Mystery cold,
　　To thee have they told
Secrets the years may yet unfold!

Sorrow of night,
　　Is love so light
As to come and go like a breeze's flight!

Opiate balm,
Is death so calm
As to faint in one's ear like a distant psalm ?

XXXVII.

WINTER CLOUD.

O NAMELESS Fear, which I would fain
contemn!
The swarthy wood-marge, skeleton'd with snow
Driv'n by a sharp north-east on bough and stem:
The broad white moor, and sable stream below
Blurr'd with grey smoke-wreaths wandering to
and fro;
That monstrous cloud pressing the night on them.
Cloud without shape or colour, drooping slow
Down all the sky, and chill sleet for its hem:—
Such face of earth and time have I not watch'd
In other years: why now my spirit sinks,
Like captive who should hear, in helpless links,
Some gate of horror stealthily unlatch'd.
Who shows me? but Calamity methinks
Is creeping nigh, her cruel plot being hatch'd.

XXXVIII.

EVENING PRAYER.

GOOD Lord, to thee I bow my head;
　　Protect me sleeping in my bed;
May no ill dream disturb the night,
Nor sinful thought my soul affright;
And sacred slumbers wrap me round,
　　As with a guardian-angel's wings,
From every earthly sight and sound;
While sweetest influence, like the dew
　　Upon thine outer world of things,
Prepares a morning fresh and new.

XXXIX.

A VERNAL VOLUNTARY.

COME again, delightful Spring,
  Hasten. if you love us;
Let your woodbine-garland swing,
  Vault the blue above us!

Nay, already she is here:
  Stealthy laughters quiver
Through the ground, the atmosphere,
  Wood, and bubbling river.

Sweet the herald westwind blows.
Green peeps out from melting snows;
Snowdrop-flow'r. and crocus, dawn
With daffodil around the lawn;
Their bushy rods the sallows gild;
The clamorous rooks begin to build,

Watch the farmer dig and sow
In his miry fields below,
Gravely follow in the furrows
Picking where his plough unburrows.
Pearl-white lambkins frisk and bleat
Or kneeling tug the kindly teat:
The roguish rat is creeping nigh
His darksome cavern; low and high,
Through sun-gleam or soft rainy gloom,
Like children coursing every room
Of a new house, the swallows glance,
Wafted over Spain and France
From the sultry solemn Nile's
Mysterious lakes of crocodiles,
And the desert-lion's roar,
To a greener gentler shore.
Native lark from stair to stair
Of brilliant cloud and azure air
Mounts to the morning's top, and sings
His merry hymns on trembling wings,
Tireless, till the cressets high
Twinkle down from cooler sky.
What beholds he on this earth?
A rising tide of love and mirth.

—And was it I who lately said,
" Mirth is fled, and Love is dead,"
For chill and darkness on the day,
As on my weak and weary spirit lay ?

Welcome, every breeze and show'r:
   Sun that courts the blossom ;
Every new delicious flow'r
   Heap'd for Maia's bosom !

Every bird !—no bird alone,
   Always two together :
Spring inspiring every tone,
   Flushing every feather.

Verdure 's tufted on the briar
Like crockets of a minster-spire :
Free sprouts the youngling corn ; a light
Is on the hills ; dim nooks grow bright
With primrose-buds : with scent and sight
And song, the childhood of the year
Renews our own ; we see and hear,
We drink the fragrance, as of yore,—
A gleam, a thrill, a breath, no more.

Away, dull musing! who are these
Under the fresh-leaved linden trees?
Three favourite Children of the Spring,
Who lightly run, as half on wing,
Dorothy, Alicia, Mary;
Over moorlands wide and airy,
Deep in dells of early flow'rs,
They have been abroad for hours,
Flow'rs themselves, and fairer yet
Than primrose, windflow'r, violet,
Or even June's wild-rose to come.
Frost never touch their opening bloom
The tender fearless life to check!
—Alicia's hat is on her neck,
With flying curls and glowing face
And ringing laugh, she wins the race;
Her eyes were made for sorrow's cure,
And doubts of Heav'n to reassure.
Veils of fresh and fragrant rain
Sinking over the green plain,
Founts of sunny beams that lie
Scatter'd through the vernal sky,
The million-fold expanding woods,
Are less delightful than these children's moods.

'Tis not life, to pine and cloy;
Sickness utters treason;
Best they live, who best enjoy
Every good in season.

Glad, with moisten'd eyes, I learn
April's own caressing:
Children, every month in turn
Bring you three a blessing!

XL.

A GRAVESTONE.

FAR from the churchyard dig his grave,
  On some green mound beside the wave:
To westward, sea and sky alone,
And sunsets. Put a massy stone,
With mortal name and date, a harp
And bunch of hawthorn, carven sharp:
Then leave it free to winds that blow,
And patient mosses creeping slow,
And wandering wings, and footstep rare
Of human creature pausing there.

XLI.

ANGELA.

AFTER the long bitter days, and night-
weigh'd down with my sadness,
Faint I lay on the sofa with soften'd thoughts in a
twilight.
Stilly she glided in, and tenderly came she beside
me.
Putting her arm round my head that was weary
with sorrowful aching;
Whispering low, in a voice trembling with love and
with pity,
" Knowest thou not that I love thee?--am I not
one in thy sorrow?
" Maze not thy soul in dark windings, joy that our
Father exceds us,
" Since with his power extends the High One's
care and compassion.

" Fear not the losing of love; love is the surest of
all things,
" Heaven the birth-place and home of everything
holy and lovely.
" Go thou fearlessly on, unswerving from shades
in thy pathway;
" Pits and crags they seem, thou wilt find them
nothing but shadows.
" Take thou care of the present, thy future will
build itself for thee.
" Life in the body is full of entanglements, harsh
contradictions;
" Keep but the soul-realities, all will unwind itself
duly.
" Think of me, pray for me, love me,—I cease not
to love thee, my dearest."

So it withdrew and died. The heart, too joyful,
too tender,
Felt a new fear of its pain, and its want, and the
desolate evening
Sunken, and dull, and cold. But quickly a kind
overflowing

Soothed my feverish eyelids: my spirit grew
    calmer and calmer:
Noting, at length, how the gloom acknowledged a
    subtle suffusion,
Veiling with earnest peace the stars looking in
    through the window,—
Where, at the time appointed from numberless
    millions of ages,
Slowly, up eastern night, like a pale smoke
    mounted the moon-dawn.

XLII.

THE MOWERS.

1.

WHERE mountains round a lonely dale
    Our cottage-roof enclose,
Come night or morn, the hissing pail
    With yellow cream o'erflows;
And roused at break of day from sleep,
    And cheerly trudging hither,—
A scythe-sweep, and a scythe-sweep,
    We mow the grass together.

2.

The fog drawn up the mountain-side
    And scatter'd flake by flake,
The chasm of blue above grows wide,
    And richer blue the lake;

Gay sunlights o'er the hillocks creep,
  And join for golden weather,—
A scythe-sweep, and a scythe-sweep,
  We mow the dale together.

3.

The goodwife stirs at five, we know,
  The master soon comes round,
And many swaths must lie a-row
  Ere breakfast-horn shall sound:
The clover and the fiorin deep,
  The grass of silvery feather,—
A scythe-sweep, and a scythe-sweep,
  We mow the dale together.

4.

The noon-tide brings its welcome rest
  Our toil-wet brows to dry:
Anew with merry stave and jest
  The shrieking hone we ply.
White falls the brook from steep to steep
  Among the purple heather,—
A scythe-sweep, and a scythe-sweep,
  We mow the dale together.

5.

For dial, see, our shadows turn;
   Low lies the stately mead:
A scythe, an hour-glass, and an urn—
   All flesh is grass, we read.
To-morrow's sky may laugh or weep,
   To Heav'n we leave it whether:
A scythe-sweep, and a scythe-sweep,
   We've done our task together.

XLIII.

DOGMATISM.

" THUS it is written."—Where? Oh, where!
    In the blue chart of the air?
In the sunlight? in the dark?
In the distant starry spark?
In the white scroll of the cloud?
In the waved line of the flood?
In the forms of peak or cliff,
In the rock's deep hieroglyph?
In the scribbled veins of metal?
In the tracings on the petal?
In the fire's fantastic loom?
In the fur, or scale, or plume?
In the greeting brother's glance?
In the corpse's countenance?
In men's real thoughts and ways?
Time's long track, or passing days?

In the cipher of the whole ?
In the core of my own soul ?
Nay !--I have sincerely sought,
But no glimpse of this thing caught.

XLIV.

ÆOLIAN HARP.

HEAR you now a throbbing wind that calls
Over ridge of cloud and purple flake !
Sad the sunset's ruin'd palace-walls,
Dim the line of mist along the lake,—
Even as the mist of Memory.
O the summer-nights that used to be !

An evening rises from the dead
Of long-ago (ah me, how long !)
Like a story, like a song,
Told, and sung, and pass'd away.
Love was there, that since hath fled,
Hope, whose locks are turn'd to grey,
Friendship, with a tongue of truth,
And a beating heart of youth,
Wingèd Joy, too, just alighted,
Ever-welcome, uninvited :

Love and Friendship, Hope and Joy,
With arms about each-other twined,
Merrily watching a crescent moon,
Slung to its gold nail of a star,
Over the fading crimson bar,
Like a hunter's horn: the happy wind
Breathed to itself some twilight tune,
And bliss had no alloy.

Against the colours of the west
Trees were standing tall and black:
The voices of the day at rest,
Night rose around, a solemn flood,
With fleets of worlds: and our delightful mood
Rippled in music to the rock and wood;
Music with echoes, never to come back.
The touch upon my hand is this alone—
A heavy tear-drop of my own.

Listen to the breeze: " O loitering Time !-
" Unresting Time !—O viewless rush of Time !"
Thus it calls and swells and falls,
From sunset's wasted palace-walls,
And ghostly mists that climb.

XLV.

AMONG THE HEATHER.

(AN IRISH SONG.)

1.

ONE evening walking out, I o'ertook a modest
colleen,
When the wind was blowing cool, and the harvest
leaves were falling.
" Is our road, by chance, the same? Might we
travel on together?"
" O, I keep the mountain side, (she replied) among
the heather."

2.

" Your mountain air is sweet when the days are
long and sunny,
When the grass grows round the rocks, and the
whinbloom smells like honey;

" Colleen," young girl.

But the winter 's coming fast, with its foggy,
    snowy weather,
And you 'll find it bleak and chill on your hill,
    among the heather."

3.

She praised her mountain home : and I 'll praise it
    too, with reason,
For where Molly is, there 's sunshine and flow'rs
    at every season.
Be the moorland black or white, does it signify a
    feather,
Now I know the way by heart, every part, among
    the heather ?

4.

The sun goes down in haste, and the night falls
    thick and stormy ;
Yet I 'd travel twenty miles to the welcome that 's
    before me ;
Singing hi for Eskydun, in the teeth of wind and
    weather !
Love 'll warm me as I go through the snow, among
    the heather.

XLVI

TWO MOODS.

1.

SLOW drags this dreary season:
   The earth a lump of lead:
The vacant skies, blue skies or brown,
   Bereft of joy and hope.
I cannot find a reason
   To wish I were not dead,
Unfasten'd and let slide, gone down
   A dumb and dusky slope.
I recognize the look of care
In every face; for now I share
What makes a forehead wrinkles wear,
   And sets a mouth to mope.

A sombre, languid yearning
   For silence and the dark:

Shall wish, or fear, or wisest word,
 Arouse me any more?
 What profits bookleaf-turning?
 Or prudent care and cark?
Or Folly's drama, seen and heard
 And acted as before?
No comfort for the dismal Day:
It cannot weep, or work, or pray;
A feeble pauper, sad and grey,
 With no good thing in store.

2.

 What lifts me and lightens?
 Enriches and brightens
The day, the mere day, the most marvellous day!
 O pleasure divine!
 An invisible wine
Pours quick through my being; broad Heaven is
 benign,
And the Earth full of wonders, and both of them
 mine.—
 What first shall I do, shall I say?
See the bareheaded frolicsome babes as they run
Go skipping from right foot to left foot in fun,—

'Tis the pleasure of living;
Too long I've o'erlook'd it,
In sulk and misgiving,
And lunatic fret;
But it wakes in me yet,
Though the world has rebuked it:
O city and country! O landscape and sun!
Air cloudy or breezy,
And stars, every one!
Gay voices of children!
All duties grown easy,
All truths unbewild'ring,
Since Life, Life immortal, is clearly begun!

XLVII.

MEA CULPA.

AT me one night the angry moon,
Suspended to a rim of cloud,
Glared through the courses of the wind.
Suddenly then my spirit bow'd
And shrank into a fearful swoon
That made me deaf and blind.

We sinn'd—we sin—is that a dream?
We wake—there is no voice nor stir;
Sin and repent from day to day,
As though some reeking murderer
Should dip his hand in a running stream,
And lightly go his way.

Embrace me, fiends and wicked men,
For I am of your crew.   Draw back,
Pure women, children with clear eyes.
Let Scorn confess me on his rack,—

Stretch'd down by force, uplooking then
Into the solemn skies !

Singly we pass the gloomy gate :
Some robed in honour, full of peace,
Who of themselves are not aware,
Being fed with secret wickedness,
And comforted with lies : my fate
Moves fast ; I shall come there.

With all so usual, hour by hour,
And feeble will so lightly twirl'd
By every little breeze of sense,—
Lay'st thou to heart this common world !
Lay'st thou to heart the Ruling Power,
Just, infinite, intense ?

Thou wilt not frown, O God. Yet we
Escape not thy transcendent law :
It reigns within us and without,
What earthly vision never saw
Man's naked soul may suddenly see,
Dreadful, past thought or doubt.

XLVIII

DOWN ON THE SHORE.

1.

DOWN on the shore, on the sunny shore !
  Where the salt smell cheers the land ;
Where the tide moves bright under boundless light,
  And the surge on the glittering strand ;
Where the children wade in the shallow pools,
  Or run from the froth in play ;
Where the swift little boats with milk-white wings
  Are crossing the sapphire bay,
And the ship in full sail, with a fortunate gale,
  Holds proudly on her way.
Where the nets are spread on the grass to dry,
And asleep, hard by, the fishermen lie,
Under the tent of the warm blue sky,
With the hushing wave on its golden floor
  To sing their lullaby.

2.

Down on the shore, on the stormy shore!
  Beset by a growling sea.
Whose mad waves leap on the rocky steep
  Like wolves up a traveller's tree.
Where the foam flies wide, and an angry blast
  Blows the curlew off, with a screech :
Where the brown sea-wrack, torn up by the roots,
  Is flung out of fishes' reach ;
Where the tall ship rolls on the hidden shoals,
  And scatters her planks on the beach.
Where slate and straw through the village spin.
And a cottage fronts the fiercest din
With a sailor's wife sitting sad within,
Hearkening the wind and water's roar,
  Till at last her tears begin.

XLIX.

TO THE NIGHTINGALES.

1.

YOU sweet fastidious Nightingales!
The myrtle blooms in Irish vales,
By Avondhu and rich Lough Lene,
Through many a grove and bowerlet green,
Fair-mirror'd round the loitering skiff.
The purple peak, the tinted cliff,
The glen where mountain-torrents rave
And foliage blinds their leaping wave,
Broad emerald meadows fill'd with flow'rs.
Embosom'd ocean-bays are ours
With all their isles; and mystic tow'rs
Lonely and grey, deserted long,—
Less sad if they might hear that perfect song!

2.

What scared ye? (ours, I think, of old)
The sombre Fowl hatch'd in the cold?

King Henry's Normans, mail'd and stern,
Smiters of galloglas and kern?
Or, most and worst, fraternal feud,
Which sad Ierne long hath rued?
Forsook ye, when the Geraldine,
Great chieftain of a glorious line,
Was hunted on his hills and slain,
And one to France and one to Spain,
The remnant of the race withdrew?
Was it from anarchy ye flew,
And fierce oppression's bigot crew,
Wild complaint, and menace hoarse,
Misled, misleading voices, loud and coarse?

3.

Come back, O Birds,—or come at last!
For Ireland's furious days are past;
And, purged of enmity and wrong,
Her eye, her step, grow calm and strong.
Why should we miss that pure delight?
Brief is the journey, swift the flight;

"Galloglas."—"kern."—Irish foot-soldier; the first heavy-
armed, the second light.

And Hesper finds no fairer maids
In Spanish bow'rs or English glades,
No loves more true on any shore,
No lovers loving music more.
Melodious Erin, warm of heart,
Entreats you;—stay not then apart,
But bid the Merles and Throstles know
(And ere another May-time go)
Their place is in the second row.
Come to the west, dear Nightingales!
The Rose and Myrtle bloom in Irish vales.

L.

THESE little Songs,
  Found here and there.
Floating in air
By forest and lea,
Or hill-side heather.
In houses and throngs,
Or down by the sea,
Have come together,
How, I can't tell:
But I know full well
No witty goose-wing
On an inkstand begot 'em.
Remember each place
And moment of grace,
In summer or spring,
Winter or autumn,

By sun, moon, stars,
Or a coal in the bars,
In market or church,
Graveyard or dance,
When they came without search,
Were found as by chance.
A word, a line,
You may say are mine;
But the best in the songs,
Whatever it be,
To you, and to me,
And to no one belongs.

THE END.

LONDON: PRINTED BY WHITTINGHAM AND WILKINS,
TOOKS COURT, CHANCERY LANE.

186, FLEET STREET,
Jan. 1865.

MESSRS. BELL AND DALDY'S
NEW AND STANDARD PUBLICATIONS.

RS. GATTY'S PARABLES FROM NATURE;
with Notes on the Natural History. The Four Series complete in one Volume. Illustrated by W. Holman Hunt, Otto Speckter, C. W. Cope, R.A., E. Warren, W. Millais, G. Thomas, P. H. Calderon, A. R. A., Lorenz Fröhlich, B. Foster, E. B. Jones, H. Weir, J. Tenniel, J. Wolf, W. P. Burton, M. E. Edwards, and Chas. Keene. Imp. 8vo., ornamental cloth, 21s.

FIRST AND SECOND SERIES, 16 Illustrations. 10s. 6d.

THIRD AND FOURTH SERIES, 15 Illustrations. 10s. 6d.

THE CUSTOMS AND TRADITIONS OF PALESTINE.
Illustrating the Manners of the Ancient Hebrews. By Dr. E. Pierotti, Author of "Jerusalem Explored." 9s.

THE ENTIRE WORKS OF THE LATE J. W. GILBART,
uniformly printed in 6 vols. 8vo.   [*In the Press.*

A VOLUME OF SERMONS BY THE RIGHT REV. G. J.
MOUNTAIN, D.D., LATE BISHOP OF QUEBEC.   [*In the Press.*

ECLOGÆ LATINÆ. A New Elementary Latin Reading Book.
By the Rev. Percival Frost, late Fellow of St. John's College, Cambridge.   [*In the Press.*
This volume is arranged like the " Analecta Græca Minora," it has a Lexicon at the end, and is graduated so that the pupil after passing through it may take up Ovid or Cæsar.

FIFTY MODERN POEMS, BY W. ALLINGHAM, Author
of " Day and Night Songs," and " Laurence Bloomfield."   [*In the Press.*

JERUSALEM EXPLORED; being a Description of the Ancient
and Modern City, with upwards of One Hundred Illustrations, consisting
of Views, Ground-plans, and Sections. By Dr. Ermete Pierotti, Doctor
of Mathematics, Architect-Engineer to His Excellency Soorraya Pasha
of Jerusalem, and Architect of the H ly Land. (Translated by the Rev.
T. G. Bonney, M.A., Fellow of St. John's College, Cambridge.) 2 vols.
Impl. 4to. *5l. 5s.*

**THE "ARTIST'S EDITION" OF WASHINGTON
IRVING'S** SKETCH-BOOK. Small 4to., with 220 Illustrations.
31s. 6l.

**FAC-SIMILES OF ORIGINAL STUDIES BY MICHAEL
ANGELO,** in the University Galleries, Oxford. Etched by Joseph
Fisher. 4to., half in roxco. 21s.

**FAC-SIMILES OF ORIGINAL STUDIES BY RAF-
FAELLE,** in the University Galleries, Oxford. Etched by Joseph
Fisher, with Introduction and Descriptions. Proof before letter, 31. 3s.

These volumes give faithful representations of this matchless Collection of Drawings, made by the late Sir Thomas Lawrence, and purchased by the University for 7000.

THE IMPERIAL ELZEVIR SHAKESPEARE. Edited by
Mr. Keightley. In two handsome Volumes, printed at the Chiswick
Press on the finest paper, with best Steel ornaments. Imp. 8vo. 15s.

THE GNOSTICS AND THEIR REMAINS, Ancient and
Mediæval. By C. W. King, M.A., Author of "Antique ...". ...
8vo. 12s.

LAYS OF THE WESTERN GAEL, and other Poems. By
Samuel Ferguson, Author of "The Forging of the Anchor," Crown
8vo. 7s.

**AFTERNOON LECTURES ON LITERATURE AND
ART,** delivered in ... during ... ...
Crown 8vo. ... ...

THE FIRST SERIES ON ENGLISH LITERATURE. 5s.

ANTHOLOGIA LATINA. A Selection of choice Latin
Poetry, with Notes, by Rev. Lewis Campbell, Assistant Master
Eton College ... 5s.

CHURCH DOCTRINE—BIBLE TRUTH. By Rev. M. F.
Sadler, Author of "The Second Adam" ... and "The Sacrament of ..." 3l. 6s.

THE ELOHISTIC AND JEHOVISTIC THEORY MI-
NUTELY EXAMINED, with some remarks on Scripture and Science.
By the Rev. Edward Bincy, late Fellow of Clare College, Cambridge.
[In the Press.

DRYDEN'S POETICAL WORKS. Aldine Edition. With
Memoir, by the Rev. R. Hooper, F.S.A. Carefully revised. 5 vols.
[Shortly.

COWPER'S POETICAL WORKS, including his Translations.
A New Edition. Edited, with Memoir, by John Bruce, Esq., F.S.A. 3
vols. *[In the Press.*

HOST AND GUEST: a Book about Dinners, Wines, and
Desserts. By A. V. Kirwan, of the Middle Temple, Esq. Crown 8vo. 9s.

ALEXANDER HAMILTON AND HIS CONTEMPORA-
RIES; or, the Rise of the American Constitution. By C. J. Rieth-
ar, Esq., Author of "Teuton," a Poem, and "Frederick Lucas,"
an Essay. Crown 8vo. 10s. 6d.

A HISTORY OF THE INTELLECTUAL DEVELOPMENT
OF EUROPE. By John William Draper, M.D., LL.D. 2 vols. 8vo.
14s.

THE DECLINE OF THE ROMAN REPUBLIC. By Ge
..... M.A. 8vo. Vol. I. 15s. Vol. II. 7s. 6d.

THE BOOK OF PSALMS: a New Translation, with Introductions and Notes, Critical and Expository. By the Rev. J. J.
Stewart Perowne, Editor and Translator of Langston's Commentary and Exposition of the Epistle to the Romans. 8vo. Vol. I. 14s.

PICTURES: AND OTHER POEMS. By Thomas Ashe.
Foolscap 8vo. 5s.

HOUSEHOLD DEVOTIONS; or, Family Prayers for the
Weeks of the Year. By Lewis Hensley, M.A., Vicar of Hurstmonceux, late
Fellow of Trinity College, Cambridge. Crown 8vo. 6s. 6d.

SHORTER HOUSEHOLD DEVOTIONS. By the same
Author. 18mo. 1s.

SHORT MEDITATIONS for Every Day in the Year. Edited by the Very Rev. the Dean of Chichester. *New Edition, revised and corrected.* 2 vols. Fcap. 8vo. 11s.

THE BOOK OF COMMON PRAYER. Ornamented with Head-pieces and Initial Letters specially designed for this edition. Printed in red and black at the Cambridge University Press. 24mo. Best morocco. 10s. 6d. Also in ornamental bindings, at various prices.

A large paper Edition, crown 8vo. Best morocco, 18s. Also in ornamental bindings, at various prices.

BRITISH SEAWEEDS. Drawn from Professor Harvey's "Phycologia Britannica," with Descriptions in popular language by Mrs. Alfred Gatty. 4to. 2l. 5s.

This volume contains drawings of the British Seaweeds in 80 figures, coloured after nature, with descriptions of each, including all the newly discovered species; an Introduction, an Amateur's Synopsis, Rules for preserving and laying out Seaweeds, and the Order of their arrangement in the Herbarium.

BRITISH BEETLES. Transferred in 250 plates from Curtis's "British Entomology," with Descriptions by E. W. Janson, Registrar of the Entomological Society, &c. 1vo. Cloth gilt, 1l. 1s. 0d.

NEW VOLUMES OF BELL AND DALDY'S
ELZEVIR SERIES.

BURNS'S SONGS. With the Copyright Pieces purchased by the late Mr. Pickering for the Aldine Edition. 1s. 6d.

WALTON'S ANGLER. Frontispiece, 4s. 6d. *[Ready.*

WASHINGTON IRVING'S SKETCH-BOOK. *Portrait.* 5s.

WASHINGTON IRVING'S TALES OF A TRAVELLER. 5s.

MILTON'S PARADISE LOST. *[Preparing.*

SHAKESPEARE. Edited by T. Keightley. 6 vols. 5s. each.

**ELL and DALDY'S POCKET VOLUMES.** A Series of Select Works of Favourite Authors, adapted for general reading, moderate in price, compact and elegant in form, and executed in a style fitting them to be permanently preserved. 32mo.

Ready.

Walton's Lives of Donne, Wotton, Hooker, &c. 3s.

Burns's Poems. 2s. 6d.

Burns's Songs. 2s. 6d.

Washington Irving's Sketch Book. 3s.

Walton's Complete Angler. Illustrated. 2s. 6d.

Sea Songs and Ballads. By Charles Dibdin and others. 2s. 6d.

White's Natural History of Selborne. 3s.

Coleridge's Poems. 2s. 6d.

The Robin Hood Ballads. 2s. 6d.

The Midshipman.—Sketches of his own early Career, by Capt. Basil Hall, R.N., F.R.S.

The Lieutenant and Commander. By the same Author. 3s.

Southey's Life of Nelson. 2s. 6d.

Longfellow's Poems. 2s. 6d.

Lamb's Tales from Shakspeare. 2s. 6d.

George Herbert's Poems. 2s.

George Herbert's Remains. 1s. 6d

George Herbert's Works. 3s.

Milton's Paradise Lost. 2s. 6d.

Milton's Paradise Regained and other Poems. 2s. 6d.

Preparing.

Gray's Poems.

Goldsmith's Poems.

Goldsmith's Vicar of Wakefield.

Henry Vaughan's Poems.

And others.

In cloth, top edge gilt, at 6d. per volume extra; in half morocco, Roxburgh style, at 1s. extra; in antique or best plain morocco at 4s. 6d. extra.

ELL and DALDY'S ELZEVIR SERIES OF STANDARD AUTHORS. Small fcap. 8vo.

Messrs. BELL and DALDY, having been favoured with many requests that their Pocket Volumes should be issued in a larger size, so as to be more suitable for Presents and School Prizes, have determined upon printing New Editions in accordance with these suggestions.

They will be issued under the general title of "ELZEVIR SERIES," to distinguish them from their other collections. This general title has been adopted to indicate the spirit in which they will be prepared, that is to say, with the greatest possible accuracy as regards text, and the highest degree of beauty that can be attained in the workmanship.

They will be printed at the Chiswick Press, on fine paper, with rich borders, and will be issued in tasteful binding at prices varying from 6d.

Burns's Poems, price 4s. 6d. ⎱ *These editions contain all the copyright*
Burns's Songs, price 4s. 6d. ⎰ *pieces published by the late Mr. Pickering in the Aldine Edition.*

Longfellow's Poems, price 4s. 6d.

Coleridge's Poems, price 4s. 6d.

Walton's Angler, price 4s. 6d.

Walton's Lives, price 5s.

Irving's Sketch Book, price 5s.

Shakespeare's Plays. Carefully edited by Thomas Keightley. In . . vols. Price 5s. each.

Milton's Paradise Lost. 5s.

Milton's Paradise Lost.   *Preparing.*

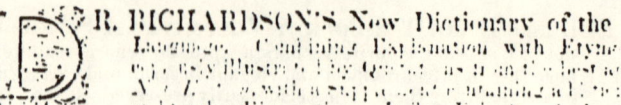

R. RICHARDSON'S New Dictionary of the English
Language, Combining Explanation with Etymology, and
copiously illustrated by Quotations from the best authorities.
New Edition, with a Supplement containing additional Words
and further Illustrations. In two Vols. 4to. 4*l*. 14*s*. 6*d*. Half-
bound in russia, 5*l*. 15*s*. 6*d*. Russia, 6*l*. 12*s*.

The Words—with those of the same Family—are traced to their
Origin.

The Explanations are deduced from the Primitive Meaning through
the various Uses.

The Quotations are arranged Chronologically, from the Earliest
Period to the Present.

. The Supplement, separately, 12*s*.

An 8vo. Edition, without the Quotations," Half-bound in Russia, ...

"It is an admirable companion for Literary ....
the reference ....
it ....
knowledge ....
all inquirers .... The ....
....

Dr. Richardson on the Study of Language: an Exposition of
Horne Tooke's Diversions of Purley. Post 8vo. 5*s*. 6*d*.

The Library of English Worthies.

A Series from the works of our Authors, carefully edited, printed
to correspond with the Aldine Poets, and illustrated by portraits
of the Worthies, drawn in Outline.

SPENSER'S Complete Works: with Life, Notes, ...
.... A .... Five Vols. 30*s*.

HERBERT'S Poems. Remains: S. T. Coleridge,
.... L ....

J. .... Angler. By .... 2 Vols.

L .... H. W. L.

The Aldine Edition of the British Poets.

AKENSIDE'S Poetical Works, with Memoir by the Rev. A. Dyce, and additional Letters, carefully revised. 5s. Morocco, or antique morocco, 10s. 6d.

Collins's Poems, with Memoir and Notes by W. Moy Thomas, Esq. 3s. 6d. Morocco, or antique morocco, 8s. 6d.

Gray's Poetical Works, with Notes and Memoir by the Rev. John Mitford. 5s. Morocco, or antique morocco, 10s. 6d.

Kirke White's Poems, with Memoir by Sir H. Nicolas, and additional notes. Carefully revised. 5s. Morocco, or antique morocco, 10s. 6d.

Shakespeare's Poems, with Memoir by the Rev. A. Dyce. 5s. Morocco, or antique morocco, 10s. 6d.

Young's Poems, with Memoir by the Rev. John Mitford, and additional Poems. 2 vols. 10s. Morocco, or antique morocco, 1l. 1s.

Thomson's Poems, with Memoir by Sir H. Nicolas, annotated by Peter Cunningham, Esq., F.S.A., and additional Poems, carefully revised. 2 vols. 10s. Morocco, or antique morocco, 1l. 1s.

Thomson's Seasons, and Castle of Indolence, with Memoir. 6s. Morocco, or antique morocco, 11s. 6d.

Dryden's Poetical Works, with Memoir by the Rev. R. Hooper, F.S.A. Carefully revised. 5 vols. *In the Press.*

Cowper's Poetical Works, including his Translations. Edited, with Memoir, by John Bruce, Esq., F.S.A. 3 vols. *[Nearly.]*

Uniform with the Aldine Edition of the Poets.

The Works of Gray, edited by the Rev. John Mitford. With his Correspondence with Mr. Chute and others, Journal kept at Rome and a criticism on the opera, &c. New Edition. 5 vols. 1l. 5s.

The Temple, or Sacred Poems. By George Herbert, with Coloured Notes. New Edition. 5s. Morocco, or antique calf, 10s. 6d.

Quarles's Sacred Poems and Pious Ejaculations, with Memoir by A. B. Grosart. New Edition. 5s. Antique calf, plain. Large Paper, 7s. 6d. Antique calf, 11s. Antique morocco ...

Presentation copies of the play of George Herbert, they being less of ...

Jeremy Taylor's Rule and Exercises of Holy Living and Holy Dying ...... Morocco, or antique calf, 10s. 6d.

Butler's Analogy of Religion; with Analytical Introduction ......

Bishop Butler's Sermons and Remains; with Memoir, by the Rev. E. Steere, LL.D. 6s.

  *** This volume contains some additional remains, which are copyright, and render it the most complete edition extant.

Bishop Butler's Complete Works; with Memoir by the Rev. Dr. Steere. 2 vols. 12s.

Bacon's Advancement of Learning. Edited, with short Notes, by the Rev. G. W. Kitchin, M.A., Christ Church, Oxford. 6s.; morocco or antique calf, 11s. 6d.

Bacon's Essays; or, Counsels Civil and Moral, with the Wisdom of the Ancients. With References and Notes by S. W. Singer, F.S.A. 5s. Morocco, or antique calf, 10s. 6d.

Bacon's Novum Organum. Newly translated, with short Notes, by the Rev. Andrew Johnson, M.A. 6s. Antique calf, 11s. 6d.

Locke on the Conduct of the Human Understanding; edited by Bolton Corney, Esq., M.R.S.L. 2s. 6d. Antique calf, 8s. 6d.

  "I cannot think any parent or instructor justified in neglecting to put this little treatise into the hands of a boy about the time when the reasoning faculties become developed."—*Hallam.*

Ultimate Civilization. By Isaac Taylor, Esq. 6s.

Logic in Theology, and other Essays. By Isaac Taylor, Esq. 6s.

The Thoughts of the Emperor M. Aurelius Antoninus. Translated by George Long. 6s.

The Schole Master. By Roger Ascham. Edited, with copious Notes and a Glossary, by the Rev. J. E. B. Mayor, M.A. 6s.

DOMESTIC Life in Palestine. By M. E. Rogers. Second Edition. Post 8vo. 10s. 6d.

Servia and the Servians. By the Rev. W. Denton, M.A. With Illustrations. Crown 8vo. 8s. 6d.

The Boat and the Caravan. A Family Tour through Egypt and Syria. New Edition. With Illustrations. Post 8vo. 7s.

Fragments of Voyages and Travels. By Captain Basil Hall, R.N. 1st, 2nd, and 3rd Series, calf extra, 5s. each.

Frederick Lucas. A Biography. By C. J. Riethmüller, author of "Teuton, a Poem. Crown 8vo. 6s.

Legends of the Lintel and the Ley. By Walter Cooper Dendy. Crown 8vo. 7s.

The Gem of Thorney Island; or, The Historical Associations of Westminster Abbey. By the Rev. J. Ridgway, M.A. Crown 8vo. 7s. 6d.

Gifts and Graces. A new Tale, by the Author of "The Rose and the Lotus." Post 8vo. 7s. 6d.

The Manse of Mastland. Sketches: Serious and Humorous, in the Life of a Village Pastor in the Netherlands. Translated from the Dutch by Thomas Keightley, M.A. Post 8vo. 9s.

The Leadbeater Papers: a Selection from the MSS. and Correspondence of Mary Leadbeater, containing her Annals of Ballitore, with a Memoir of the Author; Unpublished Letters of Edmund Burke; and the Correspondence of Mrs. R. Trench and Rev. G. Crabbe. *Second Edition.* 2 vols. crown 8vo. 14s.

The Home Life of English Ladies in the Seventeenth Century. By the Author of "Magdalen Stafford." *Second Edition, enlarged.* Fcap. 8vo. Calf. 9s. 6d.

Magdalen and her Hero. By the Author of "Magdalen Stafford." 2 vols. Fcap. 8vo. 12s.

Magdalen Stafford. A Tale. Fcap. 8vo. 5s.

Mrs. ALFRED GATTY'S POPULAR WORKS.

Mrs. Gatty is ... in the art of writing for the young. She is to ... of this generation what ... Miss Edgeworth was to ...

PARABLES from Nature: a Handsomely Illustrated Edition, with Notes on the Natural History. The two Series complete in one volume. Imperial 8vo. ... Illustrations by eminent artists, ornamented cloth, gilt edges, 21s.

First and Second Series, from the above. 10s. 6d.

Third and Fourth Series, ditto. 10s. 6d.

... from Nature. 16mo, with Illustrations. First Series ...

... Realized. 16mo. *Third Edition.* 2s.

... Illustrated. 16mo, with Illustrations. ...

... Tales. Illustrated by Clara S. Lane. Fcap. 8vo. ...

A 2

Aunt Judy's Letters. Illustrated by Clara S. Lane. Fcap.
8vo. 3s. 6d.

The Human Face Divine, and other Tales. With Illustrations
by C. S. Lane. Fcap. 8vo. 3s. 6d.

The Fairy Godmothers and other Tales. *Fourth Edition.* Fcap.
8vo, with Frontispiece. 2s. 6d.

Legendary Tales. With Illustrations by Phiz. Fcap. 8vo. 5s.

The Poor Incumbent. Fcap. 8vo. Sewed, 1s. Cloth, 1s. 6d.

The Old Folks from Home; or, a Holiday in Ireland. *Second
Edition.* Fcap. 8vo. 7s. 6d.

Melchior's Dream, and other Tales. By J. H G. Edited by
Mrs. Gatty. Illustrated. Fcap. 8vo. 3s. 6d.
   "Melchior's Dream is an exquisite little Story, charming by original
humour, buoyant spirits and tender pathos."—*Athenaeum.*

By the late Mrs. Woodrooffe.

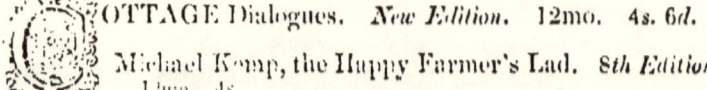

OTTAGE Dialogues. *New Edition.* 12mo. 4s. 6d.

   Michael Kemp, the Happy Farmer's Lad. *8th Edition.*
12mo. 4s.

Sequel to Michael Kemp. *New Edition.* 12mo. 6s. 6d.

THE Adventures of a Little French Boy. With 50
   Illustrations. Crown 8vo. Cloth, gilt edges. 7s. 6d.

   The Life and Adventures of Robinson Crusoe. By
   Daniel Defoe. With 100 Illustrations by E. H. Wehnert.
   Uniform with the above. Crown 8vo. Cloth, gilt edges, 7s. 6d.

Andersen's Tales for Children. Translated by A. Wehnert.
With 105 Illustrations by E. H. Wehnert, W. Thomas, and others.
Uniform with the above. Crown 8vo. Cloth, gilt edges. 7s. 6d.

Katie; or the Simple Heart. By D. Richmond, Author of
"Annie Maitland." Illustrated by M. I. Booth. Crown 8vo. 6s.

The Feasts of Camelot, with the Tales that were told there.
Arranged and retold by the Knights of King Arthur. By Mrs. T.
K. Hervey. Post 8vo. 4s. 6d.

Glimpses into Petland. By the Rev. J. G. Wood, M.A.,
with Illustrations by Coleman. Fcap. 8vo. 4s. 6d.

Miles; or, Last Nights; or, the Franklyns. By the Author of
"---- a Voyage." Fcap. 8vo. 4s. 6d.

Aground! Torn: or Torn; or, the Lost Fathers. A Tale. By
Anne Bowman, Author of "The Kangaroo," "The Boy Voyagers," &c.
With Illustrations. Crown 8vo.

Little Maggie and her Brother. By Mrs. G. Hooper, Author of
" Arbell," &c. With a Frontispiece. Fcap. 8vo. 2s. 6d.

Church Stories. Edited by the Rev. J. E. Clarke. Crown 8vo.
2s. 6d.

Cavaliers and Round Heads. By J. G. Edgar, Author of " Sea
Kings and Naval Heroes." Illustrated by Amy Butts. Fcap. 3s. 6d.

Sea-Kings and Naval Heroes. A Book for Boys. By J. G.
Edgar. Illustrated by C. K. Johnson and C. Keene. Fcap. 8vo. 3s. 6d.

The White Lady and Undine, translated from the German by the
Hon. C. L. Lyttelton. With numerous Illustrations. Fcap. 8vo. 5s. Or,
separately, 2s. 6d. each.

The Lights of the Will o' the Wisp. Translated by Lady Maxwell
Wallace. With a coloured Frontispiece. Imperial 16mo. Cloth, gilt
edges, 5s.

The Life of Christopher Columbus, in Short Words. By Sarah
Crompton. Super royal 16mo. 2s. 6d. Also an Edition for Schools, 1s.

Guessing Stories; or, the Surprising Adventures of the Man
with the Extra Pair of Eyes. A Book for Young People. By P. Rev.
Freeman. Second Edition, Super-royal 16mo. Cloth, gilt edges. 2s. 6d.

Nursery Tales. By Mrs. Motherly. With Illustrations by C.
S. Lane. Imperial 16mo. 2s. 6d. Coloured, gilt edges, 3s. 6d.

Nursery Poetry. By Mrs. Motherly. With Eight Illustrations
by C. S. Lane. Imperial 16mo. 2s. 6d. Coloured, gilt edges, 3s. 6d.

Baptista: A Quiet Story. By the Author of " The Four Sisters."
With a Frontispiece. Crown 8vo. 6s.

Arnold Delahaize; or, the Huguenot Pastor. By Francisca
Ingram Ouvry. With a Frontispiece. Fcap. 8vo. 5s.

Denise. By the Author of " Mademoiselle Mori." *New Edition.*
Crown 8vo. 6s.

A Poetry Book for Children. Illustrated with Thirty-seven
highly-finished Engravings, by C. W. Cope. R. A., Helmsley, Palmer,
Skill, Thomas, and H. Weir. *New Edition.* Crown 8vo. 2s. 6d.

Nursery Cards. Illustrated with 120 Pictures. By Ludwig
Richter and Oscar Pletsch. Imperial 16mo. Ornamental Binding. 3s. 6d.
Coloured, 6s.

Poetry for Play-Hours. By Gerda Fay. With Eight large
Illustrations. Imperial 16mo. 3s. 6d. Coloured, gilt edges, 4s. 6d.

Very Little Tales for Very Little Children. In single Syllable
of Three and Four letters. *New Edition.* Illustrated. 2 vols. 16mo. 1s. 6d.
each, or in 1 vol. 3s.

Progressive Tales for Little Children. In words of *One* and *Two*
Syllables. Forming the sequel to "Very Little Tales." *New Edition*.
Illustrated. 2 vols. 16mo. 1s. 6d. each, or in 1 vol. 3s.

Giles Witherne; or, The Reward of Disobedience. A Village
Tale for the Young. By the Rev. J. P. Parkinson, D.C.L. *Second
Edition*. Illustrated by the Rev. F. W. Mann. super-royal 16mo. 1s.
Cloth, gilt edges, 2s. 6d.

Charades, Enigmas, and Riddles. Collected by a Cantab. *Fourth
Edition*, enlarged. Illustrated. Fcap. 8vo. 2s. 6d.

Original Acrostics. By a Circle of Friends. Fcap. 8vo. 2s. 6d.

Old Nursery Rhymes and Chimes. Collected and Arranged by
a Peal of Bells. 4to, with Ornamental Binding. 5s. 6d.

The Children's Picture Book Series.

Written expressly for Young People, super-royal 16mo.

Cloth, gilt edges, price 3s. each.

BIBLE Picture Book. Eighty Illustrations. (Coloured,
7s.)

Scripture Parables and Bible Miracles. Thirty-two
Illustrations. (Coloured, 7s. 6d.)

English History. Sixty Illustrations. (Coloured, 9s.)

Good and Great Men. Fifty Illustrations. (Coloured, 9s.)

Useful Knowledge. One Hundred and Thirty Figures.

Coloured, 7s. 2s. 6d. (Coloured, gilt edges, 3s. 6d.)

Scripture Parables. By Rev. J. E. Clarke. 16 Illustrations.

Bible Miracles. By Rev. J. E. Clarke, M.A. 16 Illustrations.

Each, plain, 1s. Sixteen Illustrations.

Book of Family Crests and Mottoes, with *Four Thousand Engravings* of the Crests of the Peers, Baronets, and Gentry of England and Wales, and Scotland and Ireland. A Dictionary of M..., &c. *Tenth Edition, enlarged.* 2 vols. small 8vo. 1l. 4s.

"Perhaps the best recommendation to its utility and correctness (in the main) is, that it has been used as a work of reference in the Herald College. No wonder it sells."—*Spectator.*

Architectural Studies in France. By the Rev. J. L. Petit, M.A., F.S.A. With Illustrations from Drawings by the Author and P. H. Delamotte. Imp. 8vo. 2l. 2s.

A Few Notes on the Temple Organ. By Edmund Macrory, M.A. *Second Edition.* Super-royal 16mo. Half morocco, Roxburgh, 3s. 6d.

Scudamore Organs, or Practical Hints respecting Organs for Village Churches and small Chancels, on improved principles. By the Rev. John Baron, M.A., Rector of Upton Scudamore, Wilts. With Designs by G. E. Street, F.S.A. *Second Edition, revised and enlarged.* 8vo. 6s.

The Bell; its Origin, History, and Uses. By Rev. A. Gatty. 3s.

Practical Remarks on Belfries and Ringers. By the Rev. H. T. Ellacombe, M.A., F.A.S., Rector of Clyst St. George, Devonshire. *Second Edition,* with an Appendix on Chiming. Illustrated. 8vo. 3s.

Engravings of Unedited or Rare Greek Coins. With Descriptions. By General C. R. Fox. 4to. Part I. Europe. Part II. Asia and Africa. 7s. 6d. each.

HISTORY of England, from the Invasion of Julius Cæsar to the end of the Reign of George II., by Hume and Smollett. With the Continuation, to the Accession of Queen Victoria, by the Rev. T. S. Hughes, B.D. late Canon of Peterborough. *New Edition,* containing Historical Illustrations, Autographs, and Portraits, copious Notes, and the Author's last Corrections and Improvements. In 18 vols. crown 8vo. 4s. each.

    Vols. I. to VI. (Hume's portion), 1l. 4s.
    Vols. VII. to X. (Smollett's ditto), 16s.
    Vols. XI. to XVIII. (Hughes's ditto), 1l. 12s.

Hume, Smollett, and Hughes's History of England. *New Library Edition.* 15 vols. 8vo. 7l. 13s. 6d.

    Hume and Smollett's portion, vols. 1 to 8, 4l.
    Hughes's portion, vols. 9 to 15, 3l. 13s. 6d.

*** Copies of the 15 volume octavo edition of Hume, Smollett, and Hughes, may be had of Messrs. Bell and Daldy with continuous titles and 40 portraits without extra charge.

The Early and Middle Ages of England. By C. H. Pearson, M.A., Fellow of Oriel College, Oxford, and Professor of Modern History, King's College, London. 8vo. 12s.

A Neglected Fact in English History. By Henry Charles Coote, F.S.A. Post 8vo. 6s.

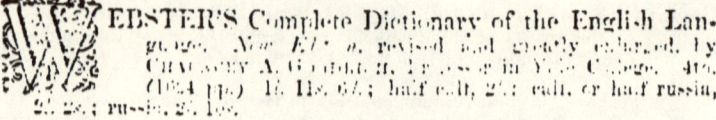

EBSTER'S Complete Dictionary of the English Language. *New Edition*, revised and greatly enlarged, by CHAUNCEY A. GOODRICH, Professor in Yale College. 4to. (1564 pp.) 1l. 11s. 6d.; half calf, 2l.; calf, or half russia, 2l. 2s.; russia, 2l. 10s.

Tables of Interest, enlarged and Improved: calculated at Five per Cent.; showing at one view the Interest of any sum, from £1 to £5000; they are also carried on by hundreds to £1000, and by thousands to £100,000, in one ready to £100,000. To which are added, Tables of Interest, from one to 12 months, and from two to 6 years. Also Tables for calculating Commission or Sales of Goods or Banking Accounts, from ½ to 5 per Cent., with several useful hints; as among which are Tables for calculating Interest on large sums for 1 day, at the several rates of 4 and 5 per Cent, to £100,000. By Joseph Kay, of Liverpool. 25th *Edition*. With a Table showing the number of days from any one day to any other day in the Year. 8vo. 1l. 1s.

The Housekeeping Book, or Family Ledger. An Improved Principle, by which an exact Account can be kept of Income and Expenditure; suitable for any Year, and may be begun at any time. With Hints on Household Management, Receipts, &c. By Mrs. Hamilton. 8vo. Cloth. 1s.; sewed, 1s.

IGHTINGALE Valley: a Collection of Choice Lyrics and Short Poems. Fifth Series of "Nightingale of the present day." Edited by W—— ——. Amalgama. Fcap. 8vo. 7s.; morocco or antique, 10s. 6d.

Legends and Lyrics, by Adelaide Anne Proctor. *Eighth Edition.* Fcap. 5s. Antique or best plain morocco, 10s. 6d.

—— *Second Series.* *Third Edition.* Fcap. 8vo. 5s.; antique or best plain morocco, 10s. 6d.

Latin Translations of English Hymns. By Charles Buchanan Pearson, M.A., Rector of ——, 8th. Fcap. 8vo. 5s.

Hymns of Love and Praise for the Church's Year. By the Rev. J. S. B. Monsell, LL.D. Fcap. 8vo. 5s.

Verses for Holy Seasons. By C. F. Alexander. Edited by the Very Rev. W. F. Hook, D.D. New Edition. Fcap. Cloth, plain *1s. 6d.*; gilt, 2s. 6d.

The Legend of the Golden Prayers, and other Poems. By the same Author. New ——, and best plain morocco, cloth, 10s. 6d.

Poems and Songs, some of which are rendered from the Spanish. By Charles Wesh Mase. Fcap. 8vo. 5s.

Ballads and Songs. By Bessie Rayner Parkes. Fcap. 5s.

The Story of Queen Isabel, and other Verses. By M. S. Author of "The Lord and others." Fcap. 8vo. 1s. 6d.

Love and Mammon, and other Poems. By F. S. Wyvill, Author of "Jessica." Fcap. 8vo. 5s.

The Fridthjof Saga. A Poem. Translated from the Norwegian. By the late G. H. ——, M.A., Rector of Dundee. Cr. 8vo. 5s. 6d.

Axel. A Poem. Translated from the Swedish. By the Rev.
R. Mucklestone, M.A., Rector of Dinedor, Herefordshire, author of a
Translation of "The Frithiof Saga," a Poem. Cr. 8vo. 2s. 6d.

Saul, a Dramatic Poem; Elizabeth, an Historical Ode; and other
Poems. By William Fullord, M.A. Fcap. 8vo. 5s.

Lays and Poems on Italy. By F. A. Mackay. Fcap. 8vo. 5s.

Poems from the German. By Richard Garnett, Author of " Io
in Egypt, and other Poems." Fcap. 8vo. 3s. 6d.

The Monks of Kilerea, and other Poems. 3rd Edition. Post. 7s. 6d.

Teuton. A Poem. By C. J. Riethmüller. Crown 8vo. 7s. 6d.

Poems, by Thomas Ashe. Fcap. 8vo. 5s.

Dryope, and other Poems. By T. Ashe. Fcap. 8vo. 6s.

Day and Night Songs; and the Music Master. A Love Poem.
By William Allingham. With nine Woodcuts, seven designed by Arthur
Hughes, one by D. G. Rossetti, and one by John E. Millais, A. R. A.
Fcap. 8vo. 5s.

David Mallet's Poems. With Notes and Illustrations by F. Dins-
dale, LL.D., F.S.A. New Edition. Post 8vo. 10s. 6d.

Ballads and Songs of Yorkshire. Transcribed from private MSS.,
rare Broadsides, and scarce Publications; with Notes and a Glossary.
By C. J. D. Ingledew, M.A., Ph.D., F.G.H.S. Fcap. 8vo. 6s.

Percy's Reliques of Ancient English Poetry. 3 vols. sm. 8vo. 15s.
Half-bound, 18s. Antique calf, or morocco, 1l. 11s. 6d.

The Book of Ancient Ballad Poetry of Great Britain. Historical,
Traditional and Romantic: with Modern Imitations, Translations, Notes
and Glossary, &c. New and Improved Edition. 8vo. Half-bound, 14s.
Antique morocco, 21s.

THIENÆ Cantabrigienses. By C. H. Cooper, F.S.A.,
and Thompson Cooper. Volume I. 1500—1585. 8vo. 18s.
Vol. II. 1586—1609. 8vo. 18s.

This work, in illustration of the biography of notable and
eminent men who have been members of the University of Cambridge,
comprises notices of:- 1. Authors. 2. Cardinals, archbishops, bishops,
abbots, heads of religious houses and other church dignitaries. 3. States-
men, diplomatists, military and naval commanders. 4. Judges and eminent practitioners of the civil or common law. 5. Sufferers for religious
or political opinions. 6. Persons distinguished for success in tuition. 7.
Eminent physicians and medical practitioners. 8. Artists, musicians,
and heralds. 9. Heads of colleges, professors, and principal officers of the
university. 10. Benefactors to the university and colleges, or to the
public at large.

Choice Notes from "Notes and Queries," by the Editor. Fcap.
8vo. 5s. each.
Vol. I.—History. Vol. II.—Folk Lore.

Master Wace's Chronicle of the Conquest of England. Translated from the Norman by Sir Alexander Malet, Bart., H.B.M. Pleni-
potentiary, Frankfort. With Photograph Illustrations of the Bayeaux
Tapestry. Medium. 4to. Half-morocco, Roxburgh, 2l. 2s.

The Prince Consort's Addresses on Different Public Occasions.
Beautifully printed by Whittingham. 4to. 10s. 6d.

Life and Books; or, Records of Thought and Reading. By J. F
Boyes, M.A. Fcap. 8vo. 5s.; calf, 8s. 6d.

Life's Problems. By Sir Rutherford Alcock, K.C.B. Second
Edition, revised and enlarged. Fcap. 5s.

Parliamentary Short-Hand (Official System). By Thompson
Cooper. Fcap. 8vo. 2s. 6d.

This is the system universally practised by the Government Official Re-
porters. It has many advantages over the system ordinarily adopted,
and has hitherto been inaccessible, except in a high-priced volume.

The Pleasures of Literature. By R. Aris Willmott, M.A. *Fifth*
Edition, enlarged. Fcap. 8vo. 5s. Morocco, 10s. 6d.

The Afternoon Lectures on English Literature. Delivered in
the Theatre of the Museum of Industry, St Stephen's Green, Dublin, in
May and June, 1863. By the Rev. James Byrne, M.A., William Lush-
ton, M.A., John K Ingram, LL.D., Arthur Houston, M.A., the Rev.
E. Whately, M.A., R. W. M'Donnell, Esq. Fcap. 8vo. 5s.

On the Influence of Mechanical and Physiological Rest in the
Treatment of Accidents and Surgical Diseases, and the Diagnostic Value
of Pain. A course of Lectures, delivered at the Royal College of Sur-
geons of England in the years 1860, 1861, and 1862. By John Hilton,
F.R.S., F.R.C.S., Member of the Council of the Royal College of Sur-
geons of England, late Professor of Anatomy and Surgery to the College,
Surgeon and Lecturer on Surgery at the University of London, &c., &c.
8vo. 18s.

By William G. T. Barter, Esq., Barrister at Law.

The Iliad of Homer literally rendered in Spenserian Stanza.
With Preface and Notes. Fcap. 8vo. 1s.

Homer and English Metre. An Essay on the Translating of the
Iliad and Odyssey. With a Literal Rendering in the Spenserian Stanza
of the First Book of the Odyssey, and Specimens of the Iliad. Crown
8vo. 6s. 6d.

Life, Law, and Literature: Essays on Various Subjects. Fcap.
8vo. 5s.

Adventures of a Summer's Eve. And other Poems. Fcap. 8vo.
6s.

Hints and Helps for Youths leaving School. By the Rev. J. S.
Gilderdale, M.A. 18mo. cloth. 2s. 6d.

Hints for Pedestrians, Practical and Medical. By G. C. Wat-
son, M.D. Third Edition, revised. Fcap. 8vo. 2s. 6d.

Hints to Maid Servants in Small Households, on Manners, Dress,
and Duties. By Mrs. Motherly. Fcap. 8vo. 1s. 6d.

A Wife's Home Duties; containing Hints to inexperienced
Housekeepers. Fcap. 8vo. 2s. 6d.

Geology in the Garden; or, The Fossils in the Flint Pebbles. With 106 Illustrations. By the Rev. Henry Eley, M.A. Fcap. 8vo. 6s.

Halcyon: or Rod-Fishing with Fly, Minnow, and Worm. To which is added a short and easy method of dressing Flies, with a description of the materials used. By Henry Wade, Honorary Secretary to the Wear Valley Angling Association. With 8 Coloured Plates, containing 117 Specimens of natural and artificial Flies, Materials, &c., and 4 Plates illustrating Fishes, Baiting, &c. Cr. 8vo. 7s. 6d.

A Handy Book of the Chemistry of Soils : Explanatory of their Composition, and the Influence of Manures in ameliorating them, with Outlines of the various Processes of Agricultural Analysis. By John Scoffern, M.B. Crown 8vo. 4s. 6d.

Flax and its Products in Ireland. By William Charley, J. P., Juror and Reporter Class XIV, Great Exhibition 1851 ; also appointed in 1862 for Class XIX. With a Frontispiece. Crown 8vo. 5s.

SERMONS.

**ARISH SERMONS.** By the Rev. M. F. Sadler, M.A., Vicar of Bridgwater. Author of "The Second Adam and the New Birth." Fcap. 8vo. Vol. I, Advent to Trinity; Vol. II, Trinity to Advent. 7s. 6d. each.

Twenty-four Sermons on Christian Doctrine and Practice, and on the Church. By C. J. Blomfield, D.D., late Lord Bishop of London. (*Hitherto unpublished.*) 8vo. 10s. 6d.

Norwich School Sermons: Preached at the Sunday Evening Service of King Edward VI. School, Norwich. By Augustus Jessopp, M.A., Head Master. Fcap. 8vo. 5s.

King's College Sermons. By the Rev. E. H. Plumptre, M.A., Divinity Professor. Fcap. 8vo. 2s. 6d.

Sermons. By the Rev. A. Gatty, D.D., Vicar of Ecclesfield. 18mo. 8s.

Twenty Plain Sermons for Country Congregations and Family Reading. By the Rev. A. Gatty, D.D., Vicar of Ecclesfield. Fcap. 5s.

Sermons Suggested by the Miracles of our Lord and Saviour Jesus Christ. By the Very Rev. Dean Hook. 2 vols. Fcap. 8vo. 12s.

Five Sermons Preached before the University of Oxford. By the Very Rev. W. F. Hook, D.D., Dean of Chichester. *Third Edition.* 3s.

Sermons, chiefly Practical. By the Rev. T. Nunns, M.A. Edited by the Very Rev. W. F. Hook, D.D., Dean of Chichester. Fcap. 8vo. 6s.

Sermons preached in Westminster. By the Rev. C. F. Secretan, M.A., Incumbent of Holy Trinity, Vauxhall-Bridge Road. Fcap. 8vo. 6s.

Sermons to a Country Congregation--Advent to Trinity. By the Rev. Hastings Gordon, M.A. 12mo. 6s.

Sermons on Popular Subjects, preached in the Collegiate Church, Wolverhampton. By the Rev. Julius Lloyd, M.A. 8vo. 4s. 6d.

The Redeemer: a Series of Sermons on Certain Aspects of the
Person and Work of our Lord Jesus Christ. By W. R. Clark, M.A.,
Vicar of Taunton. Fcap. 8vo. 5s.

The Fulness of the Manifestation of Jesus Christ: being a Course
of Epiphany Lectures. By Hezkiah Bedford Hall. B.C.L. Afternoon
Lecturer of the Parish Church, Halifax. Author of " A Companion to the
Authorized Version of the New Testament. Fcap. 8vo. 2s.

Plain Parochial Sermons. By the Rev. C. F. C. Tagott, B.A.,
late Curate of St. Michael's, Handsworth. Fcap. 8vo. 5s.

Sermons, Preached in the Parish Church of Godalming. Surrey,
by the Rev. E. J. Boyce, M.A., Vicar. Second Edition. Fcap. 8vo. 6s.

Life in Christ. By the Rev. J. Llewellyn Davies, M.A., Rector
of Christ Church, Marylebone. Fcap. 8vo. 5s.

The Church of England: its Constitution, Mission, and Trials.
By the Rt. Rev. Bishop Blomfield. Edited, with a Prefatory Memoir, by
the Ven. Archdeacon Harrison. 8vo. 10s. 6d.

Plain Sermons, Addressed to a Country Congregation. By the
late E. Blencowe, M.A. 1st and 2nd Series. 8vo. 7s. 6d. each.

Missionary Sermons preached at Hagley. Fcap. 3s. 6d.

Westminster Abbey Sermons for the Working Classes. Fcap.
1st and 2nd Series, 1858. 2s. 1859. 2s. 6d.

Sermons preached at St. Paul's Cathedral. *Authorised Edition.*
1858. Fcap. 8vo. 2s. 6d.

The Christian's Life in Heaven and on Earth. A Selection from
the Sermons of the Rev. Robert Soukey, M.A., late Fellow of Wadham,
Oxon. Fcap. 8vo. 3s.

Types of Christ in Nature. Nine Sermons preached in the Parish
Church of St. James. By the Rev. J. W. Reynolds, M.A., Incumbent
of the Parish and late Curate in Charge of the same. Fcap. 8vo. 2s. 6d.

DAILY Readings for a Year, on the Life of Our Lord and
Saviour Jesus Christ. By the Rev. Peter Young, M.A. With
Introduction by Dr. Pusey. 2 Vols. 8vo. In Antique type.

Short Sunday Evening Readings. Selected and Abridged from
various Authors by the Hon. and Rev. Canon of Canterbury. In Antique type.
8vo.

A Commentary on the Gospels for the Sundays and other Holy
Days of the Christian Year. By the Rev.

The Second Adam, and the New Birth; or, the Doctrine of Baptism as contained in Holy Scripture. By the Rev. M. F. Sadler, M.A. Vicar of Bridgewater. Author of "The Sacrament of Responsibility." *Third Edition*, greatly enlarged. Fcap. 8vo. 4s. 6d.

The Sacrament of Responsibility; or, Testimony of the Scripture to the teaching of the Church on Holy Baptism, with especial reference to the Cases of Infants, and Answers to Objections. *Sixth Edition.* 6d.

Popular Illustrations of some Remarkable Events recorded in the Old Testament. By the Rev. J. F. Dawson, LL.B., Rector of Toynton. Post 8vo. 8s. 6d.

The Acts and Writings of the Apostles. By C. Pickering Clarke, M.A. Post 8vo. Vol. 1., with Map., 7s. 6d.

A Manual for Communion Classes and Communicant Meetings. Addressed specially to the Parish Priests and Deacons of the Church of England. By C. Pickering Clarke, M.A. Fcap. 8vo. 3s. 6d.

Memoir of a French New Testament, in which the Mass and Purgatory are found in the Sacred Text; together with Bishop Kidder's "Reflections" on the same. By Henry Cotton, D.C.L., Archdeacon of Cashel. *Second Edition, enlarged.* 8vo. 3s. 6d.

The Spirit of the Hebrew Poetry. By Isaac Taylor, Esq., Author of "The Natural History of Enthusiasm," "Ultimate Civilization," &c. 8vo. 10s. 6d.

The Physical Theory of Another Life. By Isaac Taylor, Esq. Author of "Logic in Theology," "Ultimate Civilization," &c." *New Edition.* 8vo. 10s. 6d. Antique calf. 21s.

The Wisdom of the Son of David: an Exposition of the First Nine Chapters of the Book of Proverbs. Fcap. 8vo. 5s.

A Companion to the Authorized Version of the New Testament: being Explanatory Notes, together with Explanatory Observations and an Introduction. By the Rev. H. B. Hall, B.C.L. *Second and cheaper Edition,* revised and enlarged. Fcap. 8vo. 3s. 6d.

Reasons of Faith; or, the Order of the Christian Argument developed and explained. By the Rev. G. S. Drew, M.A. Fcap. 8vo. 1s. 6d.

Bishop Colenso's Examination of the Pentateuch Examined. By the Rev. G. S. Drew, Author of "Scripture Lands," "Reasons of Faith." Crown 8vo. 3s. 6d.

Charles and Josiah; or, Friendly Conversations between a Churchman and a Quaker. Crown 8vo. 5s.

Isaiah's Testimony for Jesus. With an Historical Appendix, and Copious Tabular View of the Chronology, from the Original Authorities. By W. B. Galloway, M.A., Incumbent of St. Mark's, Regent's Park, and Chaplain to the Right Hon. Viscount Hawarden. 8vo. 15s

The Divine Authority of the Pentateuch Vindicated. By Daniel
Moore, M.A., Camberwell. Crown 8vo. 6s. 6d.

Replies to the First and Second Parts of the Right Rev. the
Bishop of Natal's " Pentateuch and Book of Joshua Critically Examined."
By Franke Parker, M.A., Trinity College, Cambridge, and Rector of
Luffincott, Devon. 8vo. 9s. 6d.

Replies to the Third and Fourth Part. 8vo. 8s. 6d.

Notes and Dissertations, principally on Difficulties in the Scrip-
tures of the New Covenant. By A. H. Wratislaw, M.A., Head Master
of King Edward VI. Grammar School, Bury St. Edmunds, formerly
Fellow and Tutor of Christ's College, Cambridge. 8vo. 7s. 6d.

Readings on the Morning and Evening Prayer and the Litany.
By J. S. Blunt. *Third Edition.* Fcap. 8vo. 3s. 6d.

Confirmation. By J. S. Blunt, Author of " Readings on the
Morning and Evening Prayer," &c. Fcap. 8vo. 3s. 6d.

Life after Confirmation. By the same Author. 18mo. 1s.

Confirmation Register. Oblong 4to. Various thicknesses.
Bound in Vellum. 4s. and upwards.

A History of the Church of England from the Accession of
James II. to the Rise of the Bangorian Controversy in 1717. By the
Rev. T. Delany, M.A. 8vo. 11s.

Aids to Pastoral Visitation, selected and arranged by the Rev.
H. B. Browning, M.A., Curate of St. George, Stamford. *Second Edition.*
Fcap. 8vo. 4s. 6d.

Remarks on Certain Offices of the Church of England, popularly
termed the Occasional Services. By the Rev. W. J. Dampier. 12mo. 5s.

The English Churchman's Signal. By the Writer of " A Plain
Word to the Wise in Heart." Fcap. 8vo. 2s. 6d.

A Plain Word to the Wise in Heart on our Duties at Church, and
on our Prayer Book. *Fourth Edition.* Sewed, 1s. 6d.

The Book of Psalms (Prayer Book Version). With Short Head-
ings and Explanatory Notes. By the Rev. Ernest Hawkins, B.D., Prebendary of St. Paul's. *Second and corrected Edition, revised and enlarged,*
Fcap. 8vo. with imprest edges, 2s. 6d.

Family Prayers: containing Psalms, Lessons, and Prayers, for
every Morning and Evening in the Week. By the Rev. Ernest Hawkins,
B.D., Prebendary of St. Paul's. *Second Edition.* Fcap. 8vo. 1s.; sewed, 9d.

Household Prayers on Scriptural Subjects, for Four Weeks.
With Forms for Various occasions. By a Member of the Church of England. *Second Edition, corrected.* 8vo. 4s. 6d.

Forms of Prayer adapted to each Day of the Week. For use
in Families or Households. By the Rev. John Jebb, D.D., 8vo. 2s. 6d.

The Doctrine of Election. An Essay. By Edward Fry. Cr. 8vo.
4s. 6d.

Walton's Lives of Donne, Wotton, Hooker, Herbert, and San-
derson. A New Edition, to which is now added a Memoir of Mr. Isaac
Walton, by William Dowling, Esq. of the Inner Temple, Barrister-at-
Law. With Illustrative Notes, numerous Portraits, and other Engravings. Index, &c. Crown 8vo. 10s. 6d. Calf antique, 15s. Morocco, 18s.

The Life of Martin Luther. By H. Worsley, M.A., Rector of
Easton, Suffolk. 2 vols. 8vo. 1l. 4s.

Papers on Preaching and Public Speaking. By a Wykehamist.
Second Thousand. Fcap. 8vo. 5s.

> This volume is an enlargement and extension, with corrections, of the
> Papers which appeared in the "Guardian" in 1858-9.

The Speaker at Home. Chapters on Public Speaking and Reading
aloud by the Rev. J. J. Halcombe, M.A., and on the Physiology of Speech,
by W. H. Stone, M.A., M.B. *Second Edition.* Fcap. 8vo. 3s. 6d.

Civilization considered as a Science in Relation to its Essence, its
Elements, and its End. By George Harris, F.S.A., of the Middle Temple,
Barrister at Law, Author of "The Life of Lord Chancellor Hardwicke."
8vo. 12s.

The Church Hymnal. (with or without Psalms.) 12mo. Large
Type, 1s. 6d. 18mo. 1s. 32mo. for Parochial Schools, 6d.

> This book is now in use in every English Diocese, and is the *Authorized*
> Book in some of the Colonial Dioceses.

Church Reading: according to the method advised by Thomas
Sharp. By the Rev. J. J. Halcombe, M.A. 8vo. 8s. 6d.

The Offertory: the most excellent way of contributing Money
for Christian Purposes. By J. H. Markland, D.C.L., F.R.S., S.A. Second Edition, enlarged, 2d.

By the Rev. J. Erskine Clarke, of Derby.

HEART Music, for the Hearth-Ring: the Street-Wail;
the Country Smoke; the Work-Hour; the Rest-Day; the
Two Good-Times. New Edition, 2s.

The Giant's Arrows. A Book for the Children of
Working People. 18mo. 6d.; cloth, 1s.

In the Church. Twelve Simple Sermons. 2 vols. 1s. each;
both of them together in 1 vol. cloth, gilt, 2s.

Plain Papers on the Social Economy of the People. Fcap. 8vo.
2s.

> No. 1. Amusements of the People. No. 2. Penny Banks.—No. 3. La-
> bourers' Working Men's Associations.—No. 4. Children

The Devotional Library.

Edited by the Very Rev. W. F. HOOK, D.D., Dean of Chichester.

A Series of Works, original or selected from well-known Church of England Divines, published at the lowest price, and suitable, from their practical character and cheapness, for Parochial distribution.

SHORT Meditations for Every Day in the Year. 2 vols. (1260 pages,) 32mo. Cloth, 5s.; calf, gilt edges, 9s. Calf antique, 12s.

In Separate Parts.

ADVENT to LENT, cloth, 1s.; limp calf, gilt edges, 2s. 6d.; LENT, cloth, 9d.; calf, 2s. 3d. EASTER, cloth, 9d.; calf, 2s. 3d. TRINITY, Part I. 1s.; calf, 2s. 6d. TRINITY, Part II. 1s.; calf, 2s. 6d.

** *Large Paper Edition, revised and corrected.* 2 vols. fcap. 8vo. large type. 14s. Morocco or antique calf, 24s.

The Christian taught by the Church's Services. (490 pages), royal 32mo. Cloth, 2s. 6d.; calf, gilt edges, 4s. 6d. Calf antique, 6s.

In Separate Parts.

ADVENT TO TRINITY, cloth, 1s.; limp calf, gilt edges, 2s. 6d. TRINITY, cloth, 8d.; calf, 2s. 2d. MINOR FESTIVALS, 8d.; calf, 2s. 2d.

** *Large Paper Edition,* fcap. 8vo. large type. 6s. 6d. Calf antique, or morocco, 11s. 6d.

Devotions for Domestic Use. 32mo. cloth, 2s.; calf, gilt edges, 4s. Calf antique, 5s. 6d. Containing:—

> The Common Prayer Book the best Companion in the Family as well as in the Temple. 3d.
> Litanies for Domestic Use. 2d.
> Family Prayers; or, Morning and Evening Services for every Day in the Week. By the Bishop of Salisbury; cloth, 6d.; calf, 2s.
> Bishop Hall's Sacred Aphorisms. Selected and arranged with the Texts to which they refer. By the Rev. R. B. Exton, M.A.; cloth, 9d.

** These are arranged together as being suitable for Domestic Use; but they may be had separately at the prices affixed.

Aids to a Holy Life. First Series. 32mo. Cloth, 1s. 6d.; calf, gilt edges, 3s. 6d. Calf antique, 5s. Containing:—

> Prayers for the Young. By Dr. Hook. 1d.
> Pastoral Address to Young Communicants. By Dr. Hook. 1d.
> Helps to Self-Examination. By W. F. Hook, D.D. 1d.
> Directions for Speaking One Day Well. By Archbishop Synge. 1d.
> Rules for the Conduct of Human Life. By Archbishop Synge. 1d.
> The Sign of Christianity, wherein a short and plain Account is given of the Christian faith; Christian Duty; Christian Prayer; Christian Sacrament. By C. Ellis. 1d.
> Ejaculatory Prayer; or, the Duty of Offering up Short Prayers to God on all Occasions. By R. P. &c. 2d.
> Prayers for a Week. Second Series. 1d. 2d.
> Companion to the Church: being Prayers, thanksgivings, and Meditations. By the Rev. Dr. Hook. Cloth, 6d.

Any of the above may be had and distributed at the prices affixed; they are all of them very suitable for Young Persons and for Private Devotion.

The Devotional Library continued.

Aids to a Holy Life. Second Series. 32mo. Cloth, 2s.; calf,
gilt edges, 4s. Calf antique, 5s. 6d. Containing:—
Holy Thoughts and Prayers, arranged for Daily Use on each Day in
the Week. 3d.
The Retired Christian exercised on Divine Thoughts and Heavenly
Meditations. By Bishop Ken. 3d.
Penitential Reflections for the Holy Season of Lent, and other Days of
Fasting and Abstinence during the Year. 6d.
The Crucified Jesus; a Devotional Commentary on the XXII and
XXIII Chapters of St. Luke. By A. Horneck, D.D. 3d.
Short Reflections for every Morning and Evening during the Week.
By N. Spinckes. 2d.
The Sick Man Visited; or, Meditations and Prayers for the Sick Room.
By N. Spinckes. 5d.

*** These are arranged together as being suitable for Private Meditation and
Prayer; they may be had separately at the prices annexed.

Helps to Daily Devotion. 32mo. Cloth, 8d. Containing:—
The Sum of Christianity. 1d.
Directions for spending One Day Well, 1d.
Helps to Self-Examination. 1d.
Short Reflections for Morning and Evening. 2d.
Prayers for a Week. 2d.

The History of our Lord and Saviour Jesus Christ; in Three
Parts, with suitable Meditations and Prayers. By W. Reading, M.A.
32mo. Cloth, 2s.; calf, gilt edges, 4s. Calf antique, 5s. 6d.

Hall's Sacred Aphorisms. Selected and arranged with the Texts
to which they refer, by the Rev. R. B. Exton, M.A. 32mo. cloth, 9d.;
limp calf, gilt edges, 2s. 6d.

Devout Musings on the Book of Psalms. 2 vols. 32mo. Cloth,
gilt edges, 9s.; calf antique, 12s. Or, in four parts, price 1s.
each; limp calf, gilt edges, 2s. 6d.

The Church Sunday School Hymn Book. 32mo. cloth, 8d.; calf,
gilt edges, 2s. 6d.

** A larger Prayer Book for Prizes, &c. 1s. 6d.; calf, gilt edges, 3s. 6d.

SHORT Meditations for Every Day in the Year. Edited
by the Very Rev. W. F. Hook, D. D. New Edition, carefully
revised. 2 vols. 8vo. large type. 14s.

The Christian taught by the Church's Services. Edited
by the Very Rev. W. F. Hook, D. D. New Edition. fcap. 8vo. large type.
cloth, 5s.

Holy Thoughts and Prayers, arranged for Daily Use on each
Day, with reference to the several Hours of Prayer. By the Elton,
with a Preface. 18mo. Cloth, red edges, 2s.; calf, gilt edges, 5s.

A Companion to the Altar. Being Prayers, Thanksgivings, and
Meditations before and after the Holy Communion. Edited by the Very
Rev. W. F. Hook, D.D. New Edition. Beautifully printed in red
and black. Fcap. Cloth, red edges, 2s. Morocco, 6s.

The Church Sunday School Hymn Book. Edited by W. F.
Hook, D.D. 32mo. Cloth, 8d.; calf, gilt edges, 3s. 6d.

** For cheaper editions of these Five Books, see List of the Devotional
Library.

EDUCATIONAL BOOKS.

Bibliotheca Classica.

A Series of Greek and Latin Authors. With English Notes. 8vo. Edited by various Scholars, under the direction of G. Long, Esq., M.A., Classical Lecturer of Brighton College; and the late Rev. A. J. Macleane, M.A., Head Master of King Edward's School, Bath.

ÆSCHYLUS. By F. A. Paley, M.A. 18s.

Cicero's Orations. Edited by G. Long, M.A. 4 vols. Vol. I. 1's.; Vol. II. 14s.; Vol. III. 1's.; Vol. IV. 1's.

Demosthenes. By R. Whiston, M.A., Head Master of Rochester Grammar School. Vol. I. 16s. Vol. II.

Euripides. By F. A. Paley, M.A. 3 vols. 16s. each.

Herodotus. By J. W. Blakesley, B.D., late Fellow and Tutor of Trinity College, Cambridge. 2 vols.

Hesiod. By F. A. Paley, M.A. 10s. 6d.

Homer. By F. A. Paley, M.A. Vol. I.   *[Preparing.*

Horace. By A. J. Macleane, M.A. 18s.

Juvenal and Persius. By A. J. Macleane, M.A. 14s.

Plato. By W. H. Thompson, M.A. Vol. I.   *[Preparing.*

Sophocles. By F. H. Blaydes, M.A. Vol. I. 18s.

Terence. By E. St. J. Parry, M.A., Balliol College, Oxford. 18s.

Virgil. By J. Conington, M.A., Professor of Latin at Oxford.

Grammar-School Classics.

CÆSARIS

M. Tullii Cicero

Quinti Horatii

Juve

Grammar-School Classics continued.

P. Ovidii Nasonis Fastorum Libri Sex. By F. A. Paley. 5s.

C. Sallustii Crispi Catilina et Jugurtha. By G. Long, M.A. 5s.

Taciti Germania et Agricola. By P. Frost, M.A. 3s. 6d.

Xenophontis Anabasis, with Introduction; Geographical and other Notes, Itinerary, and Three Maps compiled from recent surveys. By J. F. Macmichael, B.A. *New Edition.* 5s.

Xenophontis Cyropaedia. By G. M. Gorham, M.A., late Fellow of Trinity College, Cambridge. 6s.

Uniform with the above.

The New Testament in Greek. With English Notes and Prefaces by J. F. Macmichael, B.A. 730 pages. 7s. 6d.

Cambridge Greek and Latin Texts.

THIS series is intended to supply for the use of Schools and Students cheap and accurate editions of the Classics, which shall be superior in mechanical execution to the small German editions now current in this country, and more convenient in form.

The texts of the *Bibliotheca Classica* and *Grammar School Classics*, so far as they have been published, will be adopted. These editions have taken their place amongst scholars as valuable contributions to the Classical Literature of this country, and are admitted to be good examples of the judicious and practical nature of English scholarship; and as the editors have formed their texts from a careful examination of the best editions extant, it is believed that no texts better for general use can be found.

The volumes will be well printed at the Cambridge University Press, in a [...] size, and will be issued at short intervals.

AESCHYLUS, ex novissima recensione F. A. Paley. 3s.

Caesar de Bello Gallico, recensuit G. Long, A.M. 2s.

Cicero de Senectute et de Amicitia et Epistolae Selectae, recensuit G. Long, A.M. 1s. 6d.

Euripides, ex recensione F. A. Paley, A.M. 3 vols. 3s. 6d. each.

Herodotus, recensuit J. W. Blakesley, S.T.B. 2 vols. 7s.

Horatius, ex recensione A. J. Macleane, A.M. 2s. 6d.

Lucretius, recognovit H. A. J. Munro, A.M. 2s. 6d.

Sallusti Crispi Catilina et Jugurtha, recognovit G. Long, A.M. 1s. 6d.

Thucydides, recensuit J. G. Donaldson, S.T.P. 2 vols. 7s.

Vergilius, ex recensione J. Conington, A.M. 3s. 6d.

Xenophontis Anabasis recensuit J. F. Macmichael, A.B. 2s. 6d.

Ciceronis Orationes. Vol. I. (Verrine Orations.) G. Long, M.A. [*In the Press.*

Juvenal and Persius. A. J. Macleane, A.M. [*In the Press.*

Novum Testamentum Graecum Textus Stephanici, 1550. Accedunt variae lectiones editionum Bezae, Elzeviri, Lachmanni, Tischendorfii, Tregellesii, curante F. H. Scrivener, A.M. 4s. 6d.

Also, on fine writing paper, for MSS. notes. Half bound, gilt top, 12s.

Foreign Classics.

With English Notes for Schools. Uniform with the GRAMMAR SCHOOL CLASSICS. Fcap. 8vo.

GERMAN Ballads from Uhland, Goethe, and Schiller, with Introductions to each Poem, copious Explanatory Notes, and Biographical Notices. Edited by C. L. Bielefeld, B.A.

Schiller's Wallenstein, complete Text. Edited by Dr. A. Buchheim, Professor of German in King's College, London. 6s.

Will also be used as a text-book for the Cambridge Middle Class Examination.

Picciola, by X. B. Saintine. Edited by Dr. Dubuc. Second Edition.

This interesting story has been selected with the intention of providing for schools and young persons . . . Experience in elementary French literature shows that those persons who care to read greatly met with a weariness of a past age.

Select Fables of La Fontaine. *Third Edition, revised.* Edited by F. Gase, M.A. 3s.

"No one need be afraid of losing time this currently French author, either on account of the . . . antiquity . . . unappreciable . . . loss . . . of the most acute . . . of the more purely . . . dread the purity of English purity . . ."

Histoire de Charles XII. par Voltaire. Edited by L. Direy. 3s. 6d.

Aventures de Télémaque, par Fénélon. Edited by C. J. Delille. 8s. 6d.

Classical Tables. 8vo.

NOTABILIA Quædam; or, the principal tenses of such irregular Greek and Latin Verbs as are . . . By Greek, Latin . . .

Greek Accidence. By the Rev. P. Frost, M.A. 1s.

Latin Accidence. By the Rev. P. Frost, M.A. 1s.

Latin Versification. 1s.

The Principles of Latin Syntax. 1s.

Greek Dialects including Homeric and Roman. By J. S. . . . M.A. . . .

A Catalogue of Greek Verbs, Irregular and Defective, with . . .

Richmond Rules for . . . Ovidian Distichs, &c. By J. Tate, M.A. . . .

AN Atlas of Classical Geography, containing 24 Maps; . . .

A Grammar School Atlas of Classical Geography. The . . .

First Classical Maps, with . . . Tables of Grecian and . . .

Analecta Graeca Minora. With Introductory Sentences, English
Notes, and a Dictionary. By the Rev. P. Frost, late Fellow of St. John's
College, Cambridge. *New Edition.* Fcap. 8vo. 3s. 6d.

Materials for Greek Prose Composition. By the Rev. P. Frost,
M.A. Fcap. 8vo. 3s. 6d. Key, 5s.

Materials for Latin Prose Composition. By the Rev. P. Frost,
M.A. *Third Edition.* 12mo. 2s. 6d. Key, 4s.

The Choephorae of Æschylus and Scholia. Revised and in-
terpreted by J. F. Davies, Esq., B.A., Trin. Coll., Dublin. 8vo. 7s. 6d.

A Latin Grammar. By T. Hewitt Key, M.A., F.R.S., Professor
of Comparative Grammar, and Head Master of the Junior School, in
University College. *Third Edition, revised.* Post 8vo. 8s.

A Short Latin Grammar, for Schools. By T. H. Key, M.A.,
F.R.S. *Third Edition.* Post 8vo. 3s. 6d.

Latin Accidence. Consisting of the Forms, and intended to pre-
pare boys for Key's Short Latin Grammar. Post 8vo. 2s.

A First Cheque Book for Latin Verse Makers. By the Rev.
F. Gretton, Stamford Free Grammar School. 1s. 6d. Key, 2s. 6d.

Reddenda; or Passages with Parallel Hints for translation into
Latin Prose and Verse. By the Rev. F. E. Gretton. Crown 8vo. 4s. 6d.

Rules for the Genders of Latin Nouns, and the Perfects and Su-
pines of Verbs; with hints on Construing, &c. By H. Haines, M.A. 1s. 6d.

Latin Prose Lessons. By the Rev. A. Church, M.A., one of the
Masters of Merchant Taylors' School. Fcap. 8vo. 2s. 6d.

The Odes and Carmen Saeculare of Horace. Translated into
English Verse by John Conington, M.A., Corpus Professor of Latin in
the University of Oxford. *Second Edition.* Fcap. 8vo. Roxburgh binding.
5s. 6d.

Quintus Horatius Flaccus. Illustrated with 50 Engravings from
the Antique. Fcap. 8vo. 5s. Morocco, 9s.

Selections from Ovid: Amores, Tristia, Heroides, Metamorphoses,
With English Notes, by the Rev. A. J. Macleane, M.A. Fcap. 8vo. 3s. 6d.

Sabrinae Corolla in hortulis Regiae Scholae Salopiensis con-
texuerunt tres viri floribus legendis. *Editio Altera.* 8vo. 12s. Morocco, 21s.

Dual Arithmetic, a New Art, by Oliver Byrne, formerly Pro-
fessor of Mathematics at the late College of Civil Engineers, Putney.
A new system of analysis of the properties of numbers. 8vo. 14s.
Copies of this analysis, with a new title page, will be supplied at 8s. 6d.
to purchasers of the former issue upon returning the old title-page to the
publishers direct, or through their booksellers.

The Elements of Euclid, Books I.—VI. XI. 1—21; XII. 1, 2;
a new text, based on that of Simson, with Exercises. Edited by H. J.
Hose, late Mathematical Master of Westminster School. Fcap. 4s. 6d.

A Graduated Series of Exercises on the Elements of Euclid:
Books I.—VI.; XI. 1—21; XII. 1, 2. Selected and arranged by Henry
J. Hose, M.A. 12mo. 1s.

The Enunciations and Figures belonging to the Propositions in
the First Six and part of the Eleventh Books of Euclid's Elements,
(usually read in the Universities,) prepared for Students in Geometry.
By the Rev. J. Brasse, D.D. *New Edition.* Fcap. 8vo, 1s. On cards,
in case, 5s. 6d.; without the Figures, 6d.

A Compendium of Facts and Formulæ in Pure and Mixed
Mathematics. For the use of Mathematical Students. By G. R.
Smalley, B.A., F.R.A.S. Fcap. 8vo. 3s. 6d.

A Table of Anti-Logarithms; containing to seven places of deci-
mals, natural numbers, answering to all Logarithms from 00001 to 99999;
and an improved table of Gauss' Logarithms, by which may be found the
Logarithm of the sum or difference of two quantities. With an Appendix,
containing a Table of Annuities for three Joint Lives at 3 per cent. Car-
lisle. By H. E. Filipowski. *Third Edition.* 8vo, 15s.

Handbook of the Slide Rule; showing its applicability to Arith-
metic, including Interest and Annuities; Mensuration, including Land
Surveying. With numerous Examples and useful Tables. By W. H.
Bayley, (late) H. M. East India Civil Service. 12mo, 6s.

Handbook of the Double Slide Rule, showing its applicability to
Navigation, including some remarks on Great Circle Sailing, with useful
Astronomical Memoranda. By W. H. Bayley. 12mo. 2s. 6d.

The Mechanics of Construction; including the Theories on the
Strength of Materials, Roofs, Arches, and Suspension Bridges. With
numerous Examples. By Stephen Fenwick, Esq., of the Royal Military
Academy, Woolwich. 8vo. 12s.

A NEW FRENCH COURSE, BY MONS. F. E. A. GASC, M.A.

FIRST French Book; being a New, Practical, and Easy
Method of Learning the Elements of the French Language.
New Edition. Fcap. 8vo, 1s. 6d.

French Fables, for Beginners, in Prose, with an Index
of all the words at the end of the work. *New Edition.* Fcap. 8vo. 2s.

Second French Book; being a Grammar and Exercise Book, on
a new and practical plan, and intended as a sequel to the "First French
Book." *New Edition.* Fcap. 8vo. 2s. 6d.

A Key to the First and Second French Books. Fcap. 8vo, 3s. 6d.

Histoires Amusantes et Instructives; or, Selections of Complete
Stories from the best French Modern Authors who have written for the
Young. With English Notes. *New Edition.* Fcap. 8vo. 2s. 6d.

Practical Guide to Modern French Conversation; containing:—
I. The most current and useful Phrases in Every-Day Talk; II. Every-
body's Necessary Questions and Answers in Travel-Talk. *New Edition.*
Fcap. 2s. 6d.

French Poetry for the Young. With English Notes, and pre-
ceded by a few plain Rules of French Prosody. Fcap. 8vo. 2s.

Materials for French Prose Composition; or, Selections from the
best English Prose Writers. With copious Foot Notes, and Hints for
Idiomatic Renderings. *New Edition.* Fcap. 8vo. 4s. 6d. Key, 6s.

Prosateurs Contemporains; or Selections in Prose, chiefly from
contemporary French Literature. With English Notes. Fcap. 8vo 5s.

Le Petit Compagnon; a French Talk-book for Little Children.
With 32 Illustrations. 16mo. 2s. 6d.

 HE French Drama ; being a Selection of the best Tragedies and Comedies of Molière, Racine, P. Corneille, T. Corneille, and Voltaire. With Arguments in English at the head of each scene, and Notes, Critical and Explanatory, by A. Gombert. 18mo. Sold separately at 1s. each. Half-bound, 1s. 6d. each.

COMEDIES BY MOLIERE.

Le Misanthrope.
L'Avare.
Le Bourgeois Gentilhomme.
Le Tartuffe.
Le Malade Imaginaire.
Les Femmes Savantes.
Les Fourberies de Scapin.

Les Précieuses Ridicules.
L'Ecole des Femmes.
L'Ecole des Maris.
Le Médecin Malgré Lui.
M. de Pourceaugnac.
Amphitryon.

TRAGEDIES, &c. BY RACINE.

La Thébaïde, ou les Frères Ennemis.
Alexandre le Grand.
Andromaque.
Les Plaideurs, (Com.)
Britannicus.
Bérénice.

Bajazet.
Mithridate.
Iphigénie.
Phèdre
Esther.
Athalie.

TRAGEDIES, &c. BY P. CORNEILLE.

Le Cid.
Horace.
Cinna.
Polyeucte.

Pompée.

BY T. CORNEILLE.
Ariane.

PLAYS BY VOLTAIRE.

Brutus.
Zaïre.
Alzire.
Oreste.

Le Fanatisme.
Mérope.
La Mort de César.
Semiramis.

Le Nouveau Trésor ; or, French Student's Companion ; designed to facilitate the Translation of English into French at Sight. *Fifteenth Edition*, with Additions. By M. E*** S*****. 12mo. Roan, 3s. 6d.

A Test-Book for Students : Examination Papers for Students preparing for the Universities or for Appointments in the Army and Civil Service, and arranged for General Use in Schools. By the Rev. Thomas Stantial, M.A., Head Master of the Grammar School, Bridgwater. Part I.—History and Geography, 2s. 6d. Part II.—Language and Literature, 2s. 6d. Part III.—Mathematical Science, 2s. 6d. Part IV.—Physical Science, 1s. 6d. Or in 1 vol., Crown 8vo., 7s. 6d.

Tables of Comparative Chronology, illustrating the division of Universal History into Ancient, Mediæval, and Modern History; and containing a System of Combinations, distinguished by a particular type, to assist the Memory in retaining Dates. By W. E. Bickmore and the Rev. C. Bickmore, M.A. *Third Edition.* 4to. 5s.

A Course of Historical and Chronological Instruction. By W. E. Bickmore. Part 2. 12mo. 3s. 6d.

**A Practical Synopsis of English History ; or, A General Summary of Dates and Events for the use of Schools, Families, and Candidates for Public Examinations. By Arthur Bowes. *Fourth Edition.* 8vo. 2s.

Under Government: an Official Key to the Civil Service, and Guide for Candidates seeking Appointments under the Crown. By J. C. Parkinson, Inland Revenue, Somerset House. *Fourth Edition.* Cr. 8vo. 3s. 6d.

The Student's Text-Book of English and General History, from B.C. 100 to the present time. With Genealogical Tables and a Sketch of the English Constitution. By D. Beale. *Second Edition.* Post 8vo. Sewed, 2s. Cloth, 2s. 6d.

Chronological Maps. By D. Beale, author of " The Text-Book of English and General History." No. 1 English, 2s. 6d. No. II. Ancient History, 2s. Or bound together in One Volume, 6d.

The Elements of the English Language for Schools and Colleges. By Ernest Adams, Ph.D., University College School, &c. &c. *Fourth Edition.* Crown 8vo. 4s. 6d.

The Geographical Text-Book: a Practical Geography, calculated to facilitate the study of that useful science, by a series of Exercises thereon. With two Maps by Sidney Hall. *New Edition.* 12mo. 2s. — Hall's Atlas of Maps complete, specially prepared for 2s. 6d.

" Manual of Book-keeping: by an Experienced Clerk. 12mo. 1s. 6d. cloth.

Double Entry Elucidated. By B. W. Foster. *Eighth Edition.* 4to. 8s. 6d.

The Young Ladies' School Register; or, Register of Studies and Conduct. 1s. 6d.

Wilson. — Thirty-nine Articles of the Church of England. With Introduction, &c. By Brooke.

Richard, Le petit Anglais; the Child's First French Book.

A School History of England, from the earliest period to the present time.

Rules for English Composition, and Poetry. By B. Brenan.

Facts, Forms, and Figures; a Series of Exercises, &c. By Pinnock.

The Child's Arithmetic, &c. By S. Barker.

The Number Primer, or First Steps in Numbers.

Natural Geography for Young Children. *New Edition.* 18mo. 2s.

Arithmetic for Young Children. By E. Hiley.

Arithmetic for Schools and Students. *Eighth Edition.* 12mo. 2s.

CLARKE'S COMMERCIAL COPY-BOOKS.
Price 4d.   A liberal allowance to Schools and Colleges.

The First Copy-Book contains *elementary turns*, with a broad mark like a T, which divides a well-formed turn into two equal parts. This exercise enables the learner to judge of *form, distance, and proportion.*

The Second contains *large-hand letters*, and the means by which such letters may be properly combined; the joinings in writing being probably as difficult to learn as the form of each character. This book also gives the whole alphabet, not in separate letters, but rather as one *word*; and, at the end of the alphabet, the difficult letters are repeated so as to render the writing of the pupil more thorough and *uniform.*

The Third contains additional *large-hand practice.*

The Fourth contains *large-hand words*, commencing with *unflourished* capitals; and the words being short, the capitals in question receive the attention they demand. As Large, and Extra Large-text, to which the fingers of the learner are not equal, have been dispensed with in this series, the popular objection of having *too many Copy-books* for the pupil to drudge through, is now fairly met. When letters are very large, the scholar cannot compass them without stopping to change the position of his hand, which *destroys* the *freedom* which such writing is intended to promote.

The Fifth contains the essentials of a useful kind of *small-hand*. There are first, as in large-hand, five easy letters of the alphabet, forming four copies, which of course are repeated. Then follows the remainder of the alphabet, with the difficult characters alluded to. The letters in this hand, especially the *a, e, d, g, o*, and *q*, are so formed that when the learner will have to correspond, his writing will not appear stiff. The copies in this book are not *more Large-hand reduced.*

The Sixth contains *small-hand copies*, with instructions as to the manner in which the pupil should hold his pen, so that when he leaves school he may not merely have some facility in copying, but really possess the information on the subject of writing which he may need at any future time.

The Seventh contains the foundation for a style of *small-hand*, adapted to females, *in briefly pointed.*

The Eighth contains copies for females; and the holding of the pen is, of course, the subject to which they specially relate.

These Series are peculiarly adapted for the ordinary purposes of commercial life. Inexpensive and when they possess the learning a fixed character suited to commercial transactions of every useful value on account. The special object of this Series of Copy-Books of such a character as such as that it ought to be used for one and again at one time by following them as far as possible, the writing is kept free and legible, whilst all needless flourishing.

CHISWICK PRESS: PRINTED BY WHITTINGHAM AND WILKINS,
TOOKS COURT, CHANCERY LANE.